Michael's Eyes

ROBERT W. FOSTER

ISBN   978-1-966473-74-9 Ebook
ISBN   978-1-966473-73-2 Hardback
ISBN   978-1-966473-72-5 Paperback

The EC Publishing LLC books may be ordered
through booksellers or by contacting:

EC Publishing LLC
116 South Magnolia Ave.
Suite 3, Unit F
Ocala, FL 34471, USA
Direct Line: +1 (352) 644-6538
Fax: +1 (800) 483-1813
http://www.ecpublishingllc.com/

Ordering Information:
Quantity sales. Special discounts are available on quantity purchases by corporations, associations, and others. For details, contact the publisher at the address above.

Printed in the United States of America

In memory of Margot

Table of Contents

Foreword vii

Introduction ix

Chapter 1   Michael's parents 1
Chapter 2   The Pharisees 3
Chapter 3   Michael's account..................................5
Chapter 4   The execution of the Galilean 22
Chapter 5   Leah's account 23
Chapter 6   The marriage 29
Chapter 7   Aaron's account...................................36
Chapter 8   Bethany...46
Chapter 9   The search for Lazarus 48
Chapter 10   The unclean made clean 51
Chapter 11   An interview with lepers......................53
Chapter 12   Jericho...56
Chapter 13   Bartimaeus..59
Chapter 14   The visitor...62
Chapter 15   The innkeeper......................................68
Chapter 16   The feeding...77
Chapter 17   The picnic...79
Chapter 18   Leah's Eyes 82
Chapter 19   Michael and Leah 85
Chapter 20   The pupil's account.............................93

Epilogue 105
About the author 107

Foreword

In the Gospels of the New Testament many characters appear only briefly, are involved somehow in Jesus' ministry, then disappear and are never heard from again. What might their lives have been like after their encounter with this extraordinary man? What could they understand about His role in the world? And for those who were the subjects of His miraculous work, how did they reconcile their experience with the fact of His execution?

We might assume that there was a general understanding of Jesus' role among the people. We are told that upon His entrance to Jerusalem for the Passover season he was met by an adoring crowd. But news of his activities could only reach people by second- or third-hand, or worse, reporting. There were no newspapers, no daily TV newscasts. There were only rumor and gossip. It is clear that many believed Him and believed *in* Him. Others did not.

I have long been fascinated by the story in the 9th chapter of John's Gospel about the beggar who had been blind from birth who miraculously received his sight. His experience, and his role in the ministry of the mysterious Gallilean, was quite different from that of others whose lives were touched by Jesus. It was not his faith that attracted Jesus to him by the road that day; it was for some other, higher reason that he was chosen.

We follow the newly sighted beggar for a while and discover the paradox of his life: He had received the most precious gift a blind man could hope for only to encounter problems as a result. He was unique in the fact that Jesus sought him out for a follow-up visit; he received new encouragement from that conversation and an indication of the purpose of it all. But what about the rest of this man's life? How did he live? And how did he reconcile his experience with the young rabbi and that man's subsequent crucifixion?

Introduction

A man with a tin cup stands by a dusty road. From time to time a passerby drops a coin into the cup; the man smiles and offers a blessing for the kindness. A group of men approach, and as they are passing one asks a philosophical question: Is this man blind because of his own sin or because of the sin of his parents? Another man in the group, who seems to be a leader, replies, then speaks to the blind man, stoops, picks something up from the ground and touches the man's sightless eyes. The blind man turns and makes his way haltingly into the city, while the group continue on their walk. It is the Sabbath.

Chapter 1

MICHAEL'S PARENTS

"You may well think it a miracle. To me it is a calamity!"

"How can you say that? The boy has a new life!"

"Yes, a new life. His new life will be more hopeless than his old life. He was a beggar, but now he is less than a beggar. He has no trade. He has no learning. He has no skills and he can no longer make his living with a tin cup. What does that mean to you? To me, as his father, it means that he must be supported, not just with a roof over his head and clothes for his back but with every crumb of bread he takes into his mouth! Who needs such a 'miracle'?"

"You speak of crumbs of food. I speak of twenty years of darkness, twenty years of depending on the alms of strangers.

"I speak of a child who has never understood his own handicap and has never complained.

"I speak as a mother whose heart was broken at his birth! Now my heart has been healed, along with his eyes.

"Where is *your* heart, husband? Where is *your* compassion? Do you recall the years you could not explain to your son the meaning of his problem or the intent of a righteous Creator, may His name be praised, who gave sightless life to this one out of thousands and with no explanation?

"Now the Master of the Universe, in His wisdom, has undone what He did. This does not impress you? You can only think of what is lost, not of what has been found. Go and cry to Moses; he will recognize your complaint, like those hopeless Hebrews who would turn back to Egypt!"

"You talk from emotion like all women. I speak from a practical point of view. There will be new hardships for the boy, yes, and for us as well. You will see. The president of the synagogue demands, not asks, *demands* that I appear and explain this thing that has happened. The city has gone crazy. People are saying the Messiah has come. Strangers are coming to our home from miles away, to see him and touch the one who was blind but now can see, as though to gain from his good fortune."

"All this talk of miracles! Look, we didn't understand how or why he was born blind and we don't understand how or why he came to see. Which event was the miracle: his blindness or his sight? As for me, his mother, I have no explanation and I will not try to invent one. Let the wise men who read Torah every day find the answers. That's what they are good at."

Chapter 2

THE PHARISEES

Rumors and reports of strange events raced throughout the city. A blind man could see! A magician had cured him. No, it was a man of G-d. Some said it was all a hoax. But other reports began to surface: A crippled man could walk, a deaf man could hear. These apparent miracles, or tricks, or imaginings of simpletons were debated and argued over in the city square and finally at the steps to the synagogue. The gathering crowd demanded an explanation from the experts in Torah. Somehow the uncommon events were connected to one man, a wandering teacher or prophet, or perhaps a fakir, but whoever he was he was stirring up the people. Most disturbing of all, he seemed to be claiming a direct connection to G-d. He was reported to have said he came from "my Father" with the clear implication of a special relationship. What did it all mean?

The Pharisees were quick to confront the issue. They had known about the "prophet" long before the blind man Michael made his fantastic claim of an instant cure. They had succeeded in ignoring reports of healing, explaining the events as the imaginings of hysterical people with no learning, who always look for miracles in order to build hope into their miserable lives. The reports had been of things happening outside the city, around the countryside, where peasants will repeat any stray tale of strange events. But now there was a man here in the city with his own claim of a miraculous cure brought about by that same nomad from Galilee people were so excited about. It was time to put an end to this public disturbance.

The simplest approach was to question Michael himself; an explanation would soon become clear. A rational approach would always put an end to rumor and false reports.

Chapter 3

MICHAEL'S ACCOUNT

Shortly after my healing the Pharisees called me to account. They are a group with little humor and less patience with the likes of me as I was in those days. Now, writing this many years later, I have a better understanding. Their authority in the synagogue was challenged by someone claiming to speak directly from G-d. The world, of course, is full of madmen who have messages from the Master of the Universe. In this case the madman was said to be performing miracles of healing, giving himself standing and credibility to claim his connection to the Blessed One. Such madness must be confronted and disproved once and for all. And I was the test case.

At first they addressed me reasonably but with condescension. They demanded that I explain my heritage: who my father was; who my father's father was and so on. I knew our family tree back for at least four generations, and I recited them by name and position. The same question was asked about my mother and her ancestry, which I answered in detail. (The benefit of blindness is the development of a memory for all kinds of abstract data and for a blind man the world is an abstraction.) Then they requested that I describe my father's position in the community, a matter well known to the elders of the synagogue, but it was clear that these experts of the Law must first authenticate my heritage and identify me as a legal Jew and as a member of the community.

Satisfied with my relationships, they started in on my condition of blindness: How long had I been blind? When did I first realize that I was blind? Was this actually blindness? Couldn't it have been a form of hysteria? Was I merely imagining my blindness? I answered patiently with a long recitation of my history from my earliest recollection. I was always blind, I explained, and there was never a time when I "realized" that I was blind. A child blind from birth cannot understand sight so is not capable of realizing the condition of blindness. I had no answer for the psychological questions at that time; I was ignorant of such concepts. I could only explain that at first I could not see but that now I see.

"If you haven't been in that position you can never understand," I told them.

After a few moments of uncomfortable silence, while the learned men searched for their next approach, one of them, much older than the others, stood up and began a new line of questioning. Now the subject was the man who was supposed to have cured me of blindness. Who was he? What did he look like? What did he say; what did he say about himself – did he claim to be a man of G-d? By the way, where is he now? the Pharisee wanted to know. I answered that I did not know who he was, not even his name. And of course I had no idea what the man looked like; *I was blind at the time!* He told me nothing about himself and made no claims for himself. In fact he hardly spoke to me at all. To me he seemed humble and kind; perhaps I was in no mood to be critical of him, as you might understand.

"As to where he is now, I have no idea. Perhaps he is performing his good works somewhere else," I said. This last was met with angry scorn by the Pharisees, whose real mood was becoming apparent.

My inquisitor finally got to the key question: What did that man do to me that I now claim he gave me my sight? My answer was brief and simple. He rubbed some mud on my eyes and sent me to the pool of Siloam to wash it off. That's all. I did what he said and I must admit that I went grudgingly, not enjoying the feeling of mud on my useless eyes. This brought some of the Pharisees to their feet, shouting that here was the final proof: the man "could not be from G-d; he does not keep the Sabbath!" But someone else argued, "how could a sinner do such miraculous signs?" At that point the meeting descended into chaos.

After a few minutes the elder of the Pharisees demanded quiet, then turned to me again. "So what do you say about the man – it was your eyes he supposedly opened?" I had begun to think these men were trying to trap me. If I said the man was from G-d I would be accused of blasphemy, settling the Pharisees' case. Perhaps I should just back down and say, no, the man did nothing for me. But I chose the middle ground, shrugged my shoulders, and suggested the man was a prophet.

Seeing they would get no acceptable explanation from me they decided to question my parents, and sent for them; so we had the second session of the inquisition.

The elder of the Pharisees, who had become the lead investigator, as it was, pointed at me and demanded to know of my parents, was this their son? If so was it true that he had been blind? And if that is so explain how it is that he can now see. My father answered very carefully, realizing his peril; he knew that anyone acknowledging the legitimacy of the man's claim would provide grounds for expulsion from the synagogue. At the same time he was compelled to be truthful and delivered his carefully prepared speech. "Yes, this is our son and yes he was blind from birth. But how he now comes to see we do not know. Ask him; he is of age and can speak for himself".

They turned to me again in their frustration. "Give glory to G-d! We know the man is a sinner!" I was even more frustrated, I must admit, and answered with some asperity, "Whether he is a sinner or not, I have no idea. One thing I do know, I was blind but now I see. The thing speaks for itself; it is what it is!" Once again they demanded to know how the man opened my eyes. Now I was really annoyed and I lost it: "I explained it to you but you did not listen! Why do you want to hear it again – do you want to be the man's disciples too!?" At this they erupted in rage and shouted at me all as one while my parents cowered in the background in wonder and fear. They had never heard me speak like this. "You are this fellow's disciple," they said. "We are disciples of Moses. We know that G-d spoke to Moses, but as for this fellow, we don't even know where he comes from!"

I was a young man at the time, merely 25 years old, with no experience in debate and with no appreciation for the politics of the religious institution. I had just experienced a life-transforming miracle without precedent in the lives of my questioners or in the history of the people of Abraham, Isaac and Jacob. I was brash and suddenly self-confident in my notoriety; I had begun to see the uniqueness of my situation and was beginning to enjoy the attention and the importance of my position. I was also tired of the harangue by these experts in the Law of Moses. And I was irritated that my father had stepped away from me in his fear for his own position. So my final sarcastic words to those Pharisees were perhaps a bit too strong.

"Now that is remarkable," I said." You don't know where he comes from, as if that made a difference. The fact is that he opened my eyes. We know that G-d does not listen to sinners; he listens to the godly man who does his will. Isn't that what you yourselves teach? Now, nobody has ever heard of opening the eyes of a man born blind. If this man were not from G-d he could do nothing!"

Having no argument left to stand on they resorted to insult, both toward me and toward my parents. They claimed I was "steeped in sin at birth," a reference to the belief that any irregularity in a child at birth was caused by the parent's sin, probably adultery and venereal disease. "How dare you lecture us," they shouted, and drove me out of the synagogue.

Nobody understands. People think they know what it means to be blind. All they have to do is close their eyes and in darkness they are experiencing blindness – they think. But that is wrong. For someone who has never had eyesight there is no sense of darkness.

There is no message of any kind, from the eyes to the brain. We have the sense of touch, the sense of hearing and of smell and taste. But there is no sense of sight. That is what people don't understand. A person born blind, with no memory of sight, lives in an empty world incomprehensible to the rest of humanity.

As an example I can tell you how hard it was for me to understand the simple business of walking. I used a stick to find my way when outside my father's house. I would feel for the edge of the road, for bumps and holes in the walkways, and to avoid trees and other objects. It was usually slow going especially if I didn't know the neighborhood. I would shuffle along, tap tapping my way. But the people around me seemed to be walking quickly, without hesitation, purposefully forging ahead. I wondered how they did that. They must have memorized every bit of the way, all the objects and barriers. And so I decided I had to work harder to store such information away in my mind. But as time passed it was always the same: everybody but me was always hurrying along while I felt my way with my stick.

My father tried to explain to me that other people could see where they were going, and so could walk quickly. "What does it mean, they can see?" I asked. As hard as my father tried to explain, it remained a mystery to me. Finally he became impatient and told me to just accept things the way they were. Understand please: it is as hard for those who see to comprehend blindness as it is for the blind to understand sight.

Mine was not an unhappy childhood, however. The terms "beg" and "beggar" were never used in our house. It was my job to be a "collector of fees" from people passing by on the road where I stood. They were to pay a kind of fee for the blessings they enjoyed. It was only later that I understood their blessing to be that they could see.

I complained once to my mother that some people would pass me by without paying the fee. She explained that neither judgment nor enforcement was my job; G-d would hold those people to account for their failures in life.

That first day by the road, when I returned home in the afternoon with my cup nearly full, I was so proud! (I suppose that people were shocked into generosity to see a five-year old, alone and begging by the road.) My brother, who was ten years older than I, worked in my father's butcher shop. Now I, too, was contributing to the family income. My father patted me on the head, that first day by the roadside, and said what a good worker I was. Nor was I unhappy to hear the other boys playing and laughing while I was out collecting. Mother had explained that their jobs were different than mine. They might play during the hours of the day while I was collecting, but later, when I came home from my job, I could play while they were working. I understood later that their "work" was the study of Torah and other schoolwork.

I had no formal schooling when I was a child; I didn't even know what school was. How could a child be expected to learn without being able to read, or to learn to read without being able to see? When my mother read to me from a book I thought she was merely reciting to me from memory. When the rabbi read the prayers in the synagogue I believed that he, too was speaking from memory. I could hold a scroll in my hands without any appreciation for it as a source of words and thoughts. When someone used the expression "to read" I took it to be a reference to recitation; I used the words read and recite interchangeably, unable to know the difference.

I received a little instruction from a patient rabbi of my father's synagogue. He devoted a few minutes of his time to me every week to teach me some of the principles of our faith, and he helped me to memorize a few of the more important prayers, and even a Psalm or two. He was wise enough to realize that I must at least know the letters and structure of the alphabet in order to speak intelligently and intelligibly. (This was a great help to me later in life, after I gained my sight.) Still, as a child, when I heard my father say the *birkat ha-mazon,* the grace after meals or the *shema,* morning and night; and when I heard the rabbi say the *tefila,* the prayers of the *mitzvah* and the *kaddish,* praising G-d: "may His great name be exalted and sanctified in the world that He created as He willed…" and so on; when I heard these prayers I could only understand that they were recited from memory, and I had to assume that the prayers were learned by the rabbi and my father from their fathers since I had no concept of the written word which could be read aloud to the congregation.

As a matter of fact there were some among the Pharisees who questioned my right even to participate in the synagogue. They recited the prophecy from the writings of Isaiah: "Go and say to this people, 'Keep listening but do not comprehend; keep looking but do not understand. Make the mind of this people dull, and stop their ears, and shut their eyes, so that they may not look with their eyes, and listen with their ears, and comprehend with their minds...'"

To these few Pharisees I was a sort of living metaphor or at least an uncomfortable reminder of Isaiah's words. Fortunately they were a minority among the leaders of the Synagogue, a bit too radical for the more moderate view by which I was looked upon with pity rather than as a prophesy-come-true.

I spent the first years of my life constructing in my mind a powerful memory. For instance, I had to memorize the words of the blessing of the *haftarah* when I was called to the Torah on the day of my *bar mitzvah*. Having gained my manhood I thought it quite natural that I recite the weekly Torah portion in the synagogue. In fact, I expected to study Torah throughout my lifetime. The rabbi had explained to me that this was the responsibility of every male Jew and I was eager to join the older boys I heard studying together, not understanding that they were reading Torah to each other, and would be reluctant to sit with me, reciting over and over, line by line so that I could memorize. It was difficult and it was slow-going for me but I progressed and by the time I gained my sight had developed my own educational preparation. That helpful rabbi taught me the words of one of the Psalms that were supposed to be a comfort to me and were a theme of my daily prayers: "Open my eyes that I may see wonderful things in your law." As puzzled as I was by the concept of seeing, which was foreign to me, none the less I repeated David's words, not with hope but with a kind of reverence for the poetry and a desire to discover wonderful things in G-d's law.

There is no preparation, however, for sudden sight for one who had been blind from birth. You might think that it is a wonderful experience. It is not. Suddenly to be aware of light – you have no idea of the shock! It is like a physical pain when your suddenly active optics begin sending crushing signals to your brain. Then there follows quickly the phenomenon of color! What is one to make of such confusion? All my life I heard people talking about red this or green that and I had no idea what the words meant. When those painful colors began to assault my brain I thought I would go mad. Nor did I know that I was looking at those concepts people had been referring to all my life: red, green, blue and worst of all yellow, the color that is like being stabbed in the eyes for the newly sighted.

The day this happened to me, when that man met me on the road, rubbed dirt on my eyes, sent me away and a few minutes later after I had washed off the dirt, I suddenly received this fifth sense in an explosion that had no reason or explanation, and I reeled about terrified and confused; when that happened to me I entered into a frightful world I didn't know and could barely believe.

Since childhood I had known the streets of my neighborhood in the City of David. I could make my way from my father's house along the dusty main road, through the square, past the market where I could smell the produce, knowing that one smell was of cabbage whose taste I knew well while another odor was a bin full of oranges that had been in the sun too long. I could tell you from the wisdom of my nose every bit of produce in the market. I would continue to make my way past the noisy stalls. I knew all the turns and corners of the streets. I hardly needed the stick I carried. I had walked this way for many years, since my father led me to the road out of the city, when I was five, and told me to stand there until he returned for me in the evening. He gave me my little tin cup to hold and told me passersby would deposit the fee and I was to bring the money home. I was to do this every day. It was to be my life's work and the only way I could contribute to the needs of the family. That routine began 20 years before and by now I knew by heart my neighborhood and the way from my father's house to my place by the road where I would beg.

But on the day I met that man and light suddenly crashed into my brain – in the first moments of sight I had no idea where I was. I was standing by the Pool of Siloam, a place in the Kidron Valley I knew well in a tactile sense. It is a sacred place believed by generations of Jews to have healing powers. My father brought me there many times in my early years, hoping for sight for his blind child. When my father gave up hope I continued to come to the place on my own. I was quite familiar with the 43 steps down to the water. But now that I could see, nothing made any sense to me. I was aware suddenly of huge objects in three dimensions, with no correlation to my perception of things. I used to run my hands along the cool stones of the walls surrounding the Pool but now as I stared at them their massive shape overwhelmed me.

Looking, I could hardly distinguish between a tree and a man – until the man moved. You must understand: I knew what a tree trunk felt like but when I saw it for the first time I did not recognize it. A blind man's perception of a tree is far from the reality of height, shade, texture and color. In those first moments I turned this way and that, bewildered and lost. I was no more than 20 minutes walk from my father's house but suddenly had no idea how to get there. Soon one of those objects I began to recognize as a man approached me. He stood in front of me for some time without speaking. Finally he said, "Michael?" How did he know my name? "Michael, are you all right? You look scared." At once I recognized the voice; this was a neighbor. For the first time in my life I looked another human being in the eyes. I spoke to him. I told him I could see him. (I think I was shouting.) He could not speak, but took several steps backward as though he himself was afraid - as though he faced a demon.

I had several such confrontations that day and it was hours before I found my way home; I will never forget meeting my mother at the front door of my father's house that day. I will never forget the look on her face when she realized I could see. Worst of all I didn't recognize her – my own mother – until she spoke. That was my first day of sight: every confrontation a shock, and there were many such confrontations.

As word got around in the city, that Michael the blind beggar could see, people came day and night for proof of this miracle. Or was it a trick? Some people are eager for miracles; others refuse to believe in an event that has no logical explanation. I had trouble with the miracle-believers who wanted to touch me as though they might feel, or share, the power of miraculous intervention. They always wanted to hold on to me - my hands or my feet - and they insisted on hearing for themselves the events of that miraculous day. Most of all they wanted to know about that man: who was he, what did he look like, what did he say to me? They wanted to know where to find him for they had miracles in mind for themselves.

The non-believers in miracles were worse. There had to be something going on here, which they would discover if only they asked the right questions:

"Is this actually Michael, the blind beggar, or is it an imposter?"

"You weren't really blind all those years, were you?"

Some said that it was just a psychological impairment caused by the trauma of birth, and I had finally, somehow, broken through the barrier to sight. That was the most popular explanation. Another, of course, was the suggestion that it was all a trick somehow, set up by my father 20 years before, to tap in to the generosity and pity of the public. Father was offended and wanted to sue for defamation of character. My mother was furious; she knew better than anyone that moments after my birth, as she held me and inspected all my parts as every mother does, that my eyes were blank, lifeless and sightless.

The nonbelievers had to have an explanation because it was plain that if I had been truly blind from birth, and a miracle had occurred, then that man must be attributed with miraculous power and was no common man. The elders of the synagogue had pronounced against such a possibility, so to believe was a repudiation of their authority. What I did not know at the time was the surge of accounts of miracles throughout the countryside. There were healings of the lame and crippled; healings of various sicknesses; and most remarkable, and most blasphemous according to the elders, was the report of a man brought forth from the tomb several days after his death!

One day a man came to our house with a proposition. He would help us to make money demonstrating "the hand of G-d among us," as he said. People wanted to see me and they wanted to hear my account of the miracle in my life. I was becoming famous. People would be willing to pay for the privilege of seeing me and witnessing this great event firsthand. He had been watching as people by the dozens were coming to our door.

What we needed, he told us, was some "order and direction" in our life. This man claimed to be a "purveyor of talent and wisdom." For instance he was, even now, preparing a form of *piyyutim* for popular presentation. This arrangement of liturgical poems, intended for religious services, could be rewritten and composed with popular themes relating to people's lives, like love and loss. He intended to put on "concerts of the *piyyutim*" for which people would pay a modest entrance fee for the entertainment. He had already identified players of wind instruments like the *uggav* and the *abbuv* who would accompany the presenters of the *piyyutim*. He would do the same for me. He would organize public readings at which I would recount my life as a beggar, born blind, followed by my telling of the sudden appearance of a man who magically gave me my sight. I would go on at great length about my dramatic journey from a life of darkness into the light of day and all its wonders. He would coach me on my presentation skills. My father would participate in order to authenticate my early condition of blindness. He might even recall the moment my mother burst into tears and cries of anguish when she discovered her newborn to be sightless. The whole wonderful, heartwarming presentation would take no more than a half hour and could be repeated in all the major cities and towns of the Judean and Samarian countryside.

It could be quite lucrative. How about it? Were we interested? My first thoughts were negative; I did not relish the idea of becoming even more of a public spectacle. My father's reaction was, predictably, more vehement. Who did this fellow think we were, circus performers? Leave that to the Romans and their Forum! And he drove the man from our house, brandishing one of his massive meat cleavers. We learned later that the man's concept of the popular *piyyutim* was met with similarly violent rejection by leaders of the Temple and the Sanhedrin.

We never heard from the "purveyor of talent and wisdom" again.

I was a simple man in those days, insensitive to the politics of the times. I knew only one thing: I had emerged from sightlessness – not mere darkness, but sightlessness – into the world of light and vision. I had no explanation for it as the Pharisees discovered on the day of my inquisition. Finally, when I stood up to them with my account and refused to discredit that man, their only solution was to put me out of the synagogue!

Later I was surprised by the re-appearance of the man who had done something to my eyes. He approached me one day shortly after my expulsion from the synagogue. I had walked out of the city, past the place where I begged for 20 years and into the countryside to be alone with my misery. It seemed to me then that this 'miracle' had only caused me new trouble. My life had not been much, but I had known who I was. My neighbors and family had accepted me with my handicap. While still blind I had brought home enough pennies most days to pay for my bread and my father had finally accepted my fate and the burden in his life that was me.

But now, with my new eyes, I was a lie to some and a wonder to others. I had no trade or occupation. I was no longer allowed to take part in the synagogue. My father, in his confusion and fear, refused to stand up to the elders in defense of my account with that man. My mother, who believed our lives had been transformed by the very power and purpose of G-d, would hardly speak to my father for what she considered to be his cowardice. Then the man came to me there near the road where we first met. I knew him at once from his voice, which was strong but gentle. He asked what my life was like since our meeting. I did not want to complain that he had done me no favor, but I told him of my problems. He spoke to me then for several minutes and there is little point in my trying to convey to you the strength of his words, but what he said to me that day was more astonishing than whatever it was he did to me at our first meeting. In the forty years I have lived since my encounter with that man I have tried to understand what happened. Nor was I able to make sense of the fate that came to him only a few days later.

During the years following my bar mitzvah, while still blind, I began to think of the future. After all, I was now a man. I would continue to earn my keep by the side of the road and I would continue to learn. It was still a mystery to me, how I was different from the other boys my age, but in my innocence I assumed I would construct a future life similar to theirs. One persistent thought began to come to me almost daily: a desire for a wife.

My older brother Aaron had married a young woman and was living in a nearby village; I often visited them in their home. It seemed to me a natural progression through life: they were living together as did our parents and I should expect to have the same experience. I spoke to my father on this subject many times as a teenager but he seemed uncomfortable speaking of about such matters. I knew something of the relationship between a husband and wife; the patient rabbi who had been instructing me had felt it necessary to make some explanation. However, my father always headed off our discussions when I brought the subject up. At first I thought he was just embarrassed to discuss the husband/wife relationship but as the years passed and I became an adult it was plain that my father had no intention of confronting the possibility of marriage for me. This, too, was a mystery to me. For my brother it was a straightforward matter. An acceptable mate had been found for him somehow, arrangements were made after some negotiations between the two sets of parents – negotiations I took to be more ceremonial than anything else – the *ketubah,* the marriage contract, was prepared and a modest (both their families were poor) wedding celebration took place. Why was I not eligible for the same experience?

Then something happened, the details of which I did not understand until much later. A cousin on my mother's side contacted my parents about another distant cousin. This young woman's parents were making contact through my mother's cousin with a tentative proposal for a union between the young woman and me. It was a circumstance of mutual handicap. The rather homely young woman was partially crippled; there was no hope that her family could make a normal match for her. Hearing of my handicap the girls' parents struck on the idea that perhaps two people, unmarriageable because of their physical conditions, would be found to be acceptable mates. It was clearly to be a marriage of desperation – a kind of last chance for these two unfortunates. None of this was explained to me though the young woman, whose name was Leah, understood. She could see and know about my condition while being fully aware of her limited appeal as a bride. I, on the other hand, was kept in the dark, literally and figuratively, about her withered leg.

As it was in my brother's case the two fathers entered into the negotiation stage except that this time it was more practical than ceremonial. The girl's father was a wealthy merchant; my father was a poor butcher. The issues of the *mohar*, the bride price, and the *shiluhim*, a dowry to be paid by the bride's father, became critical issues. In Jewish tradition the *mohar*, paid by the father of the groom to the bride's father, is meant to be a reflection of the value of the bride. The *shiluhim* on the other hand is given to equip the bride for her new life; it is her inheritance. Both fathers in this case recognized that I could never provide for a wife, especially in the style to which this young woman was accustomed. If there were to be a union her wealthy father would have to provide the means. Because of her handicap that made a conventional match impossible, it was understood that her father must be the provider. But at the same time the husband in this union had his own unique handicap. Now who owes the most in this arrangement? Which handicap was the most debilitating? Which was worse, a blind husband unable to support a family or a crippled woman unable to perform the duties of a wife?

These awkward negotiations were carried on behind closed doors over several months made more difficult by the distance between the two family's homes. My mother's cousin, who had made the first contact between the families, became the go-between, carrying proposals and counterproposals back and forth between our homes. In the end I believe that it was she who pointed out to the two stubborn fathers that this was the only realistic opportunity for the young people and incidentally, the only likely possibility for the respective families to rid themselves of the difficult situations placed upon them by an all-knowing but sometimes-capricious G-d. An agreement was finally reached only after which Leah and I were introduced to each other. We were not conscious of all the details of the marriage contract, the *ketubah*, between our fathers; our interests were confined to the prospect of finding a mate for life, a prospect less likely in Leah's thoughts than in mine. To me this was to be a normal union arranged in the usual way by the respective parents; I was as unaware of her disability as I was confused about my own. She, on the other hand, knew that she was being paired with a blind man, an arrangement thought to be equitable given her handicap.

For me that first meeting was a nervous and exciting experience. Of course, we could only have this meeting in the presence of our parents, and at subsequent meetings in the presence of a chaperone of suitably stern reliability. In spite of the peculiar circumstances surrounding these meetings Leah and I quickly became comfortable with each other. I reacted positively to her voice. She spoke softly and with a reserve I found endearing. At the time I could not gauge her reaction to me except that she did not seem to be pulling away from me as many people did who were put off by my empty eyes, who had a pervasive superstition about anyone born with such a profound handicap. After a few of these meetings a date was set for our wedding. But then I met that man by the roadside.My transformation from a blind beggar to a fully-sighted adult was so shocking to my parents that it was several days before they began to think what this might mean to my arranged wedding. My mother's first thought was how disappointed I would be faced with the reality of Leah's unfortunate condition. Surely I would object to being yoked to such a burden but worse than my reaction was her thought that her son, no longer bearing his curse, would probably never have sons of his own being burdened with a defective wife. The negotiated union no longer seemed so felicitous. As usual, my father's reaction was of the practical kind.

My father found himself caught suddenly in an arrangement quite unequal as to terms. It was no longer a matter of balancing one handicap against the other; I was no longer blind but Leah was still a cripple. Perhaps the whole dowry/bride price agreement should be re-addressed, assuming I even agreed to go forward with the wedding, an unlikely event once I saw Leah's condition, a homely, graceless cripple who would probably never bear children. So my father went back to the go-between cousin. The news of the restoration of my sight had reached her neighborhood before my father was able to relay his misgivings and like any good negotiator she had prepared her own arguments. First, she said, my father had entered into a contract and should not shame himself by withdrawing. Second, people were attributing the restoration of my sight to a miracle; my father should not cast a pall of disgrace on the young woman because of an act of G-d. Finally, what new prospect was there for me to have a career with which to support any wife, given my lack of education, training or preparation for even the most humble trade? In the face of these compelling arguments my father relented but with the caveat that should I refuse to go forward with the marriage on the basis of Leah's handicaps, which were profound, the wedding would be cancelled. Only after all this was Leah's condition revealed to me in brutal detail.

My father described to me the girl's withered leg that made it barely possible for her to walk. Worse, perhaps, was the doubt that she would ever perform normal conjugal duties, an unthinkable circumstance for a healthy young man like me in my father's consideration; in any case it seemed impossible she would bear children. I had no response to this, but the thought that Leah had suffered the same fate as I at birth gave me a sense of shared attention by the Creator who seemed to have selected us both for some extreme existence. Such was my youthful idealism, which I kept to myself knowing full well my father's tendency to an unshakable sense of logic and consistency in his world.

Next, my father told me of Leah's less-than-comely appearance. My father was sure, I believe, that I would be bitterly disappointed when I met the girl with my eyes open for the first time. I am imagining, all these years later, that my father, that day, braced himself to answer my protests at his plan to wed me to a homely cripple. What my father was never able to appreciate, however, was the effect of a lifetime of blindness in which a person does not develop normal responses to esthetics. Concepts of beauty and loveliness are never developed in such a person. Where the eyes carry no message to the brain there is no qualitative response to visual perception. A blind man forms his opinions about people from their speech rather than from their physical appearance. I had my own ideas about Leah and her character and personality based on what I could hear in her voice as well as the content of her words. I was accustomed to my mother's way of speech, which could be demanding especially in her dealings with my father, the stubborn meat cutter. My sister in law had a shrill, whiney, complaining voice; she never seemed to be quite satisfied with her life. Leah, on the other hand, spoke softly with a low timber, in an almost musical tone; I was always soothed by the sound of her voice. This effect on my spirit would not go away when I gained my sight; and we had already talked enough to recognize each other's approach to life and a common set of values.

I had no intention of canceling the wedding. x

$$\text{\raisebox{0pt}{\LARGE ❧}}$$

Chapter 4

THE EXECUTION OF THE GALILEAN

Some days after Michael had received his sight, the man who had ministered to him was executed by the authorities.

At that time Michael was still adjusting to the new sensation of vision. People were clamoring to see him and question him; his family and neighbors were excited by this miraculous event. Michael's father was trying to decide what to do about the marriage agreement with Leah's father. Michael's mother was nearly overcome emotionally; she wanted to give their small savings to the poor in thanks for this "act of G-d" as she called it. There was too much turmoil in Michael's life for him to be aware of events beyond his immediate surroundings.

The hasty trial of the Galilean and his sudden execution were unknown to Michael for several days. At the first news of what had happened Michael did not believe that the executed man could be the same person who had so dramatically changed his life. But when a more complete accounting of the event was brought to him, Michael was at first astonished, then enraged and finally filled with sorrow and disillusionment. How could this have happened? If the man was a heretic as charged, how did Michael gain his vision? What meaning could there be in the statements the Galilean made about himself?

Chapter 5

LEAH'S ACCOUNT

I weave. I have been weaving since I was seven years old. I discovered it as an activity by which I could take part in my family's daily routine. At that age I could barely stand and was still months from being able to walk very well. My parents were sure I could never do the household chores usually expected of a woman, so as a young girl I was left out of the normal practices of housekeeping, cooking and so on. One day I saw an Arab girl sitting at a primitive loom, constructing a small prayer rug that was beautiful to my eyes. For this activity I would not need strong legs. I begged my father for a loom and though nice Jewish girls in upper-class families did not ordinarily do such work, my father finally relented and found a beginner's loom for me. Twenty years later I was reasonably proficient, producing table coverings, wall hangings and modest carpets. I had become satisfied with my life. I had long since accepted my fate as a homely cripple, destined to spinsterhood, spending my days seated at my loom. I was shocked, then, when my mother suggested the possibility of marriage for me. I was not only shocked, I was frightened. I was never able to see myself as a wife. Nor could I imagine any man willing to be yoked to a woman with no desirable features. What crazy notion was this? At first I did not take the idea seriously. But my father came to me and stated quite sternly that a prospective husband had, indeed, been found and the proper negotiations were even now being conducted between the two families.

"Why are you doing this to me?" I complained. "I don't want it; I have never wanted it and I don't want it now!"

My father reasoned to me, "Leah, your mother and I are old. Soon we will be gone. We don't want you to be alone. We are doing what we think is best for you."

"But I don't want a man and no man is ever going to want me."

"You could have a life…"

"I have all the life I will ever have! I am satisfied with this life; I have learned to be satisfied. Why do you torment me now with something that can never be?"

My father was pleading now. "But it can be. There is a man. He's a man who needs you and your mother and I believe you need him."

"Why? Is he a cripple too? An old man? How can I help him? I can barely take care of myself. Or maybe he lost his arms, is that it? Between us we make up one whole person? His legs and my arms? It is grotesque! I want no part of it! Or maybe he is feeble-minded and he needs a keeper?"

"No there is nothing wrong with his arms. He is young and strong; nearly your own age. And he is of sound mind. His problem is… he is blind. He was born blind."

I could not speak. They had found someone as profoundly handicapped as me. What was I supposed to do with this proposal? I could only weep in humiliation and fury.

My father spoke very carefully to me then. "Leah, I know your ferocious determination. You bullied me into buying you that weaving equipment when you were a mere child. Against all tradition I gave in to you and your mother and hired a tutor so you could learn to read. Now, this once, trust my judgment for your best interests. Please."

Over the following days my mother reasoned with me. Finally a cousin of hers, a woman who had made the initial suggestion for this bizarre union came and spoke to me about the young man she called Michael. She described him as a fine person, rather sweet actually, according to her. Though he had spent his life begging he was a thoughtful person and bright, with an active mind. He was a student, or as much of a student as a blind man can be. He could recite long passages of Torah and was active in his father's synagogue. She was sure that he and I would get along well. We were similar in temperament. We were both patient and accepting of the lives we had been given. "At least meet him," she urged. "Give it a chance. You both deserve something better than growing old alone. The final decision will be yours; your father will not force you against your will." I was not so sure of that but I finally agreed to meet the man.

At our first meeting we sat very still for several minutes. I was studying him closely but could only imagine what was going through his mind. Why didn't he speak? We had been introduced by my mother's cousin, the putative match-maker. He nodded in my direction, then waited for me to speak. I was too dull-witted at that time to appreciate the fact that he could make no evaluation of me until he could hear me speak, while I just sat there, sizing him up. Finally the match-maker told me to speak to the man so he would at least know I was in the room!

So I tried to talk. I said hello to him. He smiled and said hello back. I waited but it was clear that he was not going to lead; he was still waiting for me. I had never been in such an awkward position. I had learned to speak when spoken to but never to venture into conversation, especially with a stranger - especially with a male stranger.

It finally dawned on me that he was the one in an awkward position; I was invisible to him. He had no idea what sort of person I was and might only develop an impression from what he could hear from me; all his impressions of a personality must come through his ears. His colorless eyes were lifeless in a face he turned first this way then that way depending on who was speaking. As I sat watching him my heart began to respond. I began to feel pity for him. What must his life be like? What could be his understanding of a world he could only judge by his sense of hearing? So I began to speak.

I told him about my home and my family. I described my parents and their activities, our neighborhood and friends. I explained that I had neither brothers nor sisters. I went on at some length spouting trivia, not knowing what else to talk about. When I paused, trying to think what to say next, Michael spoke. He said he wanted to know about me, not my family.

"Tell me about yourself," he said. But I had never talked about myself. I had always known that I was a burden to my parents and had tried to draw as little attention to myself as possible. My thoughts and opinions were of no value to anyone else. But now someone was interested and so I told him about my weaving and described some of my accomplishments, forgetting that the colors of my tapestries meant nothing to him. When I talked about the varied kinds of work I enjoyed doing he showed a real interest in the mechanics of manually constructing different types of fabrics. I explained the difference between weaving fabric on a loom, sliding the shuttlecock back and forth through the warp, or the tying of individual knots to build the nap of a carpet. He wanted to hold these things so I went to my workroom and brought several samples for his inspection. He handled the pieces carefully, seeking out the patterns – not the patterns of color but the patterns of the material itself. I could see him running his fingers carefully over the threads and knots. As I watched him I was witnessing a new concept entering into his world of darkness; I only wished that he could appreciate the color scheme of my design, of which I was quite proud.

Our early meetings took place at my father's house; my parents would not consider taking me to the humble home of a common butcher, an attitude I thought peculiar in as much as they intended for me to marry into the family. I was kept unaware of the negotiations going on between the families; I was not informed, at first, of the plan for my father to provide financially for the requirements of two people unable to provide for themselves.

It may seem strange that in our discussions during the first weeks of our "courtship" the fact that I was a cripple was never discussed. I assumed that Michael had been informed of my condition and I was unlikely to raise the subject. It was not until some years later that Michael told me that it was only after he gained his sight that he was told he had been promised to a woman who could barely walk, and, according to Michael's father, was no beauty. Michael recounted that discussion with amusement. He said it was just one more example of his father's inability to understand the concepts and values of a blind man, even those of his own son. By then I had developed confidence in our relationship. I had also been relieved of any last shred of self-consciousness about myself thanks to Michael's firm assurances of his need for me even in this new phase of his sighted life.

In the early days both the blind Michael and I, the homely girl with the withered leg, were adjusting to the possibility that we might be married and spend the rest of our lives together. We were becoming comfortable with each other. Michael seemed to accept it all as quite natural and recognized nothing strange about the program being planned by our fathers. As for me it was like something unreal. At first it was a frightening idea but as Michael and I grew more comfortable, discovering shared likes and dislikes regarding people, social situations, food, music and other experiences of life my fear began to vanish and I found myself feeling warm both toward Michael and toward the idea of a new life for myself, outside the constricting limits of my father's house. Then came the news of Michael's confrontation with a man who seemed to have given him the power of sight.

We had begun to hear rumors of a miraculous encounter of some kind of holy man and a blind man somewhere in the city several days before Michael's father brought the news to my father. There was a great deal of consternation on the part of both fathers who found themselves thrown back into the negotiation process. I was not a part of those discussions, either before or after Michael's miracle. My thoughts and feelings were not considered by the two men to be an issue of any importance. What was important to them was Michael's new condition as a "whole man", and didn't this change the conditions that led to the pre-nuptial agreements? But my thoughts had been scrambled by this news, which at first I rejected outright.

When I was forced to accept the truth of Michael's transformation I was torn between happiness for him and disappointment at the obvious thought that Michael had no interest in a crippled wife. We were no longer equal in our disabilities. I could only be a burden to Michael as I had always been to my father. It was clear to me that there would be no wedding, no marriage and I could go back to my solitary life of weaving and rug making. I tried to tell myself I was relieved.

I was surprised to hear that Michael was coming for another visit and assumed he was making an attempt at gallantry; he would explain that his new condition changed everything for him and any thought of marriage now was impossible. I would understand and graciously express my joy at his good fortune. I dreaded the meeting. It didn't go as I had expected.

Michael came into the room with an energy and exuberance I had never seen in him, smiling and almost dancing across the room. He took both my hands in his and with his warm, brown healthy eyes gazed deeply into mine and began to talk about our new life! I was astonished and speechless as the words tumbled from his mouth. We would have our home. Now he could study not only Torah, but history, philosophy and so much more. He was thankful for my father's generosity but he fully expected to earn a living for us eventually. His plan was to be a teacher, and yes, he knew he would have to catch up to the rest of the world with his study but he felt he was well prepared to embark on this exciting journey which we would travel together. And so, there was to be a wedding, to everyone's surprise. It was a surprise to everyone except Michael, that is.

Chapter 6

THE MARRIAGE

Of all the extraordinary phenomena that arrived with vision, perhaps the most astounding for Michael was discovery of the written word. Not only did he finally understand the difference between reciting and reading, but the idea of reducing sounds and words to symbols and the ability to transfer thought, in all its shifting uncertainty, to the fixed certainty of words on a page went far beyond anything he could have imagined while blind. As he made these discoveries Michael would sit for long periods of time contemplating the new wonders of communicating. He defined reading as hearing without listening. More difficult than learning to read, Michael discovered, was the art of writing, which came more slowly to him. He said that if reading was hearing without listening, then writing was speaking without talking. He was mesmerized by the graceful calligraphy of the scroll. What a wonderful invention! Had this actually been going on for centuries, and Michael was just beginning to understand it?

Michael was soon reading well and began studying Torah daily. He found part-time employment teaching young children and enjoyed their advancement with the written word that was slower than his own. With support from Leah's father they were able to have their own home and quickly adjusted to each other's habits and idiosyncrasies. Leah, too, began to enjoy studying with a new appreciation for the gift of sight. For Michael she was a source of information about the world that could come only by seeing. She brought to his attention the changing intensity of light and color as the day progressed from morning to afternoon and evening. She urged him to practice estimating distance, comparing close and distant images found in a three-dimensional world. Leah had no education in mathematics but she was able to make Michael appreciate numbers and groups of objects as more than an abstract concept. She showed him how she used color in her weaving and rug-making and how different colors worked well together, while others did not. In this she helped him to make his way in a world that was strange to him, and to appreciate the wonders of sight.

Michael was surprised by Leah's ability to read people by their facial expressions and by what she called body language. He had always been good at judging people's moods and attitudes by the sound of their speech but he discovered that even when someone in the room was silent, Leah would receive some kind of message. She remarked one night, after a joint meal with their families, that Michael's sister-in-law was unhappy about something; something was bothering her. Michael was surprised at this since his brother's wife had not spoken all evening and he had received no messages. So Leah began to tell him what to look for in people's expressions and especially how they stood or sat, and how they positioned their arms and hands. Watch their eyes, she said, and their mouths. You will almost see what they are thinking if you duplicate for yourself what you see in them. "What are we thinking when we purse our lips like this, or fold our arms across our chest, like this", she said. It was a wonder, and all very wonderful to Michael who said that Leah was like a spider sitting at the center of her web, sensing the vibrations of the people around her.

The first months in the marriage of Michael and Leah brought new experiences as their love and devotion for each other grew, as is true with most newly married young people. But for these two it was more: Michael was learning from Leah a life's worth of visual intelligence. And Leah was experiencing a vitality in her own life from Michael's dependence on her as she was guiding him through a foreign world of vision. No one had ever depended on her for anything or looked to her for advice and guidance. She realized that she was not handicapped in their relationship but had the strength and guidance her strong young husband needed and embraced gratefully. Nothing compared, however, to what she felt one day after they had been married for nearly a year, as Michael looked into her eyes and told her how beautiful she was. She suggested that the Galilean hadn't done such a good job of restoring Michael's sight if he thought her beautiful; she knew only too well that she was homely. Michael reacted to these words with unrestrained glee. "He gave me perfect vision," he said while laughing gaily, "and you are perfectly beautiful to me!"

That led them to their first serious discussion of the miracle Michael had experienced, and the man who apparently had brought it about. By this time, of course, the man was dead, having been put to death by the Romans. Nobody in Michael and Leah's society talked about him now, and few people mentioned Michael's unlikely "miracle." Others were either too frightened of the authorities to talk about it or were disillusioned and no longer hopeful for a new world order. There had actually been, for a short while, a general belief that the man was special. Some even believed that he was the Messiah. But the Messiah was supposed to free his people from the yoke of the Romans; he was going to restore the house of Jacob. Instead the man was disposed of in the most degrading way along with two common criminals.

After the Romans had killed the man, his followers went into hiding. In the months following not much was said publicly but then a new round of rumors began to circulate in the city, of a new sect who claimed the man was alive. Some even began to preach openly about the power of G-d to save sinners in the name of the man who was "rejected by his own people". Small groups of people were said to be meeting together and were actually worshiping the man as though he was G-d Himself. The Sanhedrin, the court that had prosecuted the man and had called for his death, pronounced this new group to be apostate and blasphemous. Those who would preach this "good news" publicly were vilified and attacked; one was even stoned to death in the public square.

Leah was conscious of Michael's reluctance to talk about his experience with the man but began to ask questions: What did the man say? Did his followers speak to Michael? What is Michael's opinion of the man – who was he? He had done something miraculous for Michael, so was he from G-d? How else could he have done such things? And what of the rumors going around in the city? What does it all mean?

"You ask so many questions, my Leah! But I will tell you what little I can," Michael replied. "That day, as I was begging by the road I heard a group of men approach. From their footsteps I knew there were five or six of them altogether. They started to pass by where I stood. Then, in a casual manner one of the men raised an interesting question: Why was this man blind – what had he done to deserve such a fate? Was his condition a result of his sin or was it because of something his parents had done? Another of the men, who seemed to be their leader, answered that this man's blindness was not a result of sin. Then he made a very strange statement: 'This happened,' he said, 'so that the work of G-d might be displayed in his life.' He went on talking in a riddle about the night and the day and working while he could. He described himself as 'the light of the world,' a phrase that had no meaning for me since I was unable to grasp the concept of light.

"I did not find his words comforting and resented the group's discussion of my condition as though they were conducting some kind of learned inquiry while I stood there as Exhibit A. Perhaps the man detected my resentment, though I hadn't spoken, according to that 'body language' business you talk about. He surprised me by rubbing something damp and coarse on my eyelids and spoke directly to me for the first time. He told me to go and wash in the pool of Siloam. Leah, you might think I would have been resentful at this, having dirt robbed onto my face, then being told to go and wash!

Even now when I remember the event I wonder at myself, that I was so complacent. But there was something about the man; when he spoke to you, you trusted him and did as he said. So, I went without speaking; it never occurred to me to say thank you – thank you for what? I had no idea what I was about to experience."

"That's an amazing story," Leah replied. "Surely you have an opinion about the man. What do you think? Was he a prophet? Did he come to you directly from G-d?"

Michael had no ready answer for his wife nor did he tell her of his second meeting with the man, something Michael himself did not understand. On that day he was so in awe of what had happened to him, and so moved to be in the presence of this stranger who had come into and out of his life in but a few moments, with such profound effect, he wanted to fall at the man's feet and worship him. But now the man was dead and the hopes of his followers were dead as well. But Michael's vision remained. How could he explain something to his wife that he himself did not understand?

"It is a mystery to me," Michael said after a few moments. "There is a huge contradiction in these events. A man goes about doing miraculous things for people; his own people reject him and turn him over to the despised Romans. The Romans don't seem to have a problem with the man or with what he has been doing, but out of political considerations they execute him. What am I supposed to think about all that, Leah?"

"The man's good work lives on in your own flesh," she replied. "Perhaps you have a responsibility to preserve his memory as a living testament. Perhaps you are the proof that he left behind to testify to 'the work of G-d' that he spoke of."

"Well sure, and how am I to do that? Shall I visit the members of the Sanhedrin and prove to them that they made an unfortunate mistake, by which they arranged for the execution of a man from G-d? My sessions with the leaders of our synagogue were not convincing of my 'living proof' and somehow I doubt that those learned lawyers with their long beards will be any more convinced."

"I don't know," said Leah. "And of course I don't want you to get in trouble. But it seems to me that what was done for you was done for some purpose greater than that you could look into this homely face and see beauty!"

Leah continued, "I wonder what those others are thinking – those other people who were touched by the man. Or were you the only one? We hear stories similar to yours but there has been strong denial of a series of miracles throughout the land. On the other hand if it could happen to you perhaps it happened to others, as well."

"Leah, my beloved. Are you suggesting to me that I have a responsibility to go forth, make a spectacle of myself, enter into philosophical combat with the highest court in the land, cause unrest and revolution among the people, and end up being stoned next to the Pool of Siloam where I gained my sight?"

"How you do carry on! And stop laughing at me. And you can just stop all that hugging and kissing right now! I am serious! But no, I don't want you to be a martyr. I never hoped or imagined that I would have a husband but now that I have one, even when he acts like a child, I don't want to become a widow as suddenly as I became a wife!"

The marriage was a good one and the two people were good for, and to, each other. The only question was why and how had it happened to them who had each started life with so little expectation of happiness. Leah had raised an interesting question regarding the other miracles, if there were such, performed by that man. If the rumors were true – if there were others out there somewhere, whose lives had been touched by the man – might Michael not gain a better understanding?

At first Michael tried to ignore these thoughts. His new life was good and he had no desire to embark on a quest for the truth of the matter. Why chase after answers that probably do not exist? Why enter an enterprise sure to bring grief and condemnation from The Establishment? He and Leah were happily settled; he had prospects for employment and respectability in the community; he was no longer a helpless beggar. But the questions would not leave him: what if there were others with experiences similar to his? What were their conclusions – how did they understand what had happened to them? Might he even find some explanation for the public execution of a man who only did good things among the people? Could there be purpose in the life of such a man? The more he thought about it the more he was inclined to search them out, if indeed there were such people. With Leah's encouragement he decided to try.

Chapter 7

AARON'S ACCOUNT

You ask about my brother Michael? It's a long story but I will tell you.

I was ten years old when Michael was born so I remember the day quite well. It was my first experience of the birthing process and though I am now blessed with five children of my own, at that time it was all new to me. As the day went on and I heard my mother's moans and complaints from the back room in our house, and as the midwife went in and out I watched and waited with a kind of dread. I was confused by the combination of anticipation and fear that seemed to be everywhere in our house.

My father, a meat cutter, came home from his shop several times during the day to check on my new brother's progress into the world. In late afternoon as the sky began its gray descent everything started to move more quickly. In her *puah* duties the midwife was calling for hot water while my mother's moans were turning to disturbing grunts and entreaties to the Almighty for delivery from her labor. She was no doubt in major discomfort but she called upon the words of the Psalmist with surprising strength:

"O Lord, the G-d who saves me, day and night I cry out before you. May my prayer come before you."

I was frightened; I couldn't understand what was happening.

Finally, after a crescendo of cries there was a moment of silence followed by an infant howl of complaint of a creature torn rudely from its comfort. In a loud voice the midwife announced through the closed door to the household that a son was born. My father, who had returned to the house in time for the event, broke into a psalm of thanksgiving. I remember his strong off-key voice to this day as he sang:

"Shout with joy to the Lord, all the earth! Serve the Lord with gladness; come before Him with joyful songs!"

Whenever I hear that psalm read in the meeting I am brought back to the time and place of Michael's birth and I hear again my father's triumphant, tone-deaf singing.

As my father was celebrating his manhood the midwife was performing *shifra*, the swaddling and cleaning of the infant. Of course I had no appreciation, then, for the rites and roles of midwifery according to the Talmudic sages but in my own years of fatherhood I have learned. Before the exodus of our ancestors from Egypt Pharaoh directed that the Hebrew midwives, when assisting at childbirth, should kill all the male children lest the Israelites outnumber the Egyptians. But the midwives, whose names were *Shiphra* and *Puah* refused, cleverly explaining to Pharaoh that Hebrew women are vigorous and give birth before the midwives arrive on the scene! That is why we call it *puah* when the midwife calms and encourages a woman during childbirth; and *shifra* is the cleaning-up after delivery. Apparently Michael's eyes were clenched tightly shut during the *shifra* process and the midwife made no notice of them. It wasn't until later, after my mother had regained some strength that the child was delivered into her arms. She held him in anticipation of that first mystical moment when mother and child make initial eye contact. Father and I were in an adjoining room waiting for a viewing of the child when we heard my mother's cry of agony as she discovered my brother's blank and sightless eyes. I could only think that her labor had started all over again, or that perhaps the child was dead.

In the days that followed there was an endless mourning, beating of breasts and tearing of hair and questioning of a righteous Creator, may His name be praised, who would visit such a calamity upon us. Now the only psalms I heard were the dreadful pleadings of a helpless father: "I call upon the Lord in my distress…" and "Look upon my suffering and deliver me…" and the like. My mother would not be comforted; my father stayed away from the house for long periods. The rabbi of our neighborhood synagogue was not much help, suggesting there was purpose in the Lord's judgments, seeming to suggest some fault in my parent's life. I was a forgotten member of the family for many days as I wandered about the place secretly wondering why the urchin had not just died. Look what upset this birth has brought to our lives – especially mine! Besides, what kind of life could await such a person, blind from birth?

All my mother's bitterness came to the surface when it was time for the child's *brit milah,* the ritual circumcision. In her anger she sent the *mohel* away saying that G-d had denied her therefore she would deny G-d. The poor rabbi was no match for her ferocious outbursts but he carried on stubbornly quoting the Lord's command to Moses, "This is my covenant with you and your descendants after you, the covenant you are to keep: Every male among you shall be circumcised.… For the generations to come every male among you who is eight days old must be circumcised, including those born in your household…" The rabbi's entreaties to my mother had no effect, however; she was unmoved by thoughts of the eternal covenant between G-d and His Chosen People

My mother astonished us all by challenging the rabbi. Joshua tells us, she said, that all the males born during the 40 years of our wandering in the dessert went *un*circumcised. "Well, my son whom G-d has given me will wander for his whole life like those Israelites in the dessert and like them *he will not be circumcised.*" When the rabbi protested that the boy must be circumcised in order to be a proper Jew my mother stubbornly replied, "the child was born of a Jewish mother therefore he is a Jew!" And so it was to be that my little brother began life without eyes and without the sign of his heritage in his flesh.

Rituals and signs are important to us. As a butcher's apprentice I was learning *kashrut*, the Jewish dietary law that dictates that we must deal only with beef, mutton and goat, the animals that chew their cud and have cloven hooves. I was taught that these animals must be slaughtered humanely in the *shechita* technique; the knife used to sever their throats and arteries must be smooth-edged and razor sharp in order to slice cleanly without tearing the flesh. In addition to the split-footed animals only fish equipped with scales and fins, and only birds like chickens that do not eat flesh, are permitted in the Jewish diet. All else is *treif*, whose meaning is, literally, animals that have been torn.

As a ten-year old I didn't understand the logic behind these rules but I realized only too well that all the operations carried on in my father's butchery were subject to review by the *mashgeach*, a rabbi serving as kosher watchman, who would visit our shop unannounced for his inspection, walking about peering into the corners, viewing every operation and looking suspiciously at me, expecting some clumsy contravention of the rules by this callow youth. Consequently, my father was stern and unrelenting in his instructions to me in these matters. It was not until I had apprenticed for several years that I was allowed even to handle the knives my father used. Understanding his dedication to the ancient rites and rituals you may appreciate the difficulty he had with my mother's refusal to have her son receive circumcision; the tension continued to build in our household during those first months of the boy's life.

As for me, I have to admit that the child's existence was annoying at best and an affront at worst. I felt that my own presence in the house was as though I was some impoverished, distant relative brought in to apprentice to my father. All conversation centered on the boy, his blindness, his care and feeding now, the chances of his surviving in this uncaring world later (my mother's thought) and his inability ever to provide for himself (my father's concern). To me Michael – my mother insisted we call him by his given name rather than "the kid" or "that poor creature" – was not much more than a small animal who was forever the subject of all my father's anxiety and all my mother's warmth.

My mother was determined that the boy would be treated like a normal child. He would learn to walk and speak (I doubted this) and in time would contribute to the household (highly unlikely). So she devoted herself full time to Michael's nurturing and training. There was nothing she would not do for him, though at first he was much like any infant, needing regular feeding and cleaning and changing of his soiled clothes. Needless to say I did not remember those first months in my own life when I, too, received all my mother's attention. I only knew that now I was a forgotten family member and I resented it.

I was surprised the first time I saw him haul himself to his feet. Holding on to the nearest piece of furniture he began to take a tentative step and he was soon finding his way about our house, bumping into anything in the way, falling down and getting up again. Nothing seemed to bother him or slow him down. Even then he seemed to me to be like a small clumsy animal brought into the house by my mother, all the time receiving her complete attention, having no prospect of advancement in the world while I went every day to my father's slaughter house to lift and carry large pieces of meat about, making deliveries to our customers while never receiving encouragement for my work or dedication or progress, constantly being ignored or overlooked or perhaps merely forgotten in this atmosphere of despair over the fate of a blind baby whom a righteous Creator G-d, may His name be remembered forever, had dropped into our meager existence!

I was only ten years old; perhaps you will excuse my outburst.

By his third birthday Michael was finding his way through our house with a surprising ability to remember the location of every piece of furniture – as long as I didn't rearrange things. He seemed to know exactly where the chairs and tables were placed and would weave about the place giggling happily to himself just like a real person. There was a small stepstool by my father's chair that I was able to move a few inches out of Michael's memorized route through the room. When he bumped into it a look of surprise would come to his face then he would grin as though in appreciation of the joke I had played on him.

Michael began to talk – to my surprise. It had not occurred to me that one might learn speech without being able to see, that it is through our ears, not our eyes that words bring meaning and can be repeated, even by a three-year old. I remember those days of Michael's advancement and compare them to the progress of my own children at the same age. Michael had an ability to concentrate lacking in any of my children. Perhaps blindness is an advantage to the learning process. Perhaps not being distracted by the view of the world around him Michael was able to focus on whatever lesson was before him. Even more surprising to me was that Michael never complained about his blindness, not as a small child nor later as a young adult. It was not until years afterward that Michael explained to me that a child born blind does not regret the absence of what he has never possessed.

By this time Father and Mother had begun to talk to each other again and much of their discussion was about the blind Michael and what his future might be like. As he approached his fifth year he was already showing signs of an independent nature as well as an impressive ability to learn.

My father pointed out that the only means of earning an income, for a blind man, is by begging.

At first my mother rejected the thought but finally had to admit the truth of the matter. There was no prospect of training the boy to work in Father's butchery and no other trade presented itself to my parents as a likely occupation. It was finally my mother that explained to the boy the responsibility he would have in life, to stand by the road and collect a "fee" from passersby. The fee, she explained to him, was for their right to walk freely along the dusty road into and out of our village. She pointed out to him that I, his older brother, was meeting my responsibility to contribute to the expenses of the house and preparing for my future by working with our father. Michael was to have similar responsibilities so shortly after his fifth birthday he began his career as a blind beggar: the collector of fees from travelers blessed with the power of sight.

By then I was well along in my training. I had been faithful to my Talmudic studies in preparation for my *bar mitzvah* but had concentrated on *kashrut,* the ancient law regulating the handling and preparation of meat. I was spending ten or twelve hours every day at the butchery with my father and had little time to be with my blind brother or notice his growth and advancement. I was surprised again, however, when I learned that he was meeting with old rabbi Hirschil as though he would study Torah. Then Michael began pestering me to recite the scriptures for him at the end of a day when I came home tired from hauling sides of beef. He would memorize as I would read. It became clear that Michael was actually making preparation for his future *bar mitzvah* to my amazement; and I must admit to a persistent resentment on my part. I am able to understand now, these many years later, how Michael's entrance into my world robbed me of much of my own childhood and the attention of my parents except to send me at an early age into my father's trade. Now I was expected to help Michael in his studies, to do for him what I had had to do for myself on my own time. When I finally attended his *bar mitzvah* I felt little satisfaction or pride for my blind brother who had, as everyone said, bravely overcome the cruel fate visited upon him by a "wise Master of the Universe, may His named by praised." By then I was married and living with my wife at her parents' home and was paying even less attention to Michael and his pathetic existence.

When, several years later, my father was negotiating marriage for Michael I was more than resentful. I was angry and resistant to what I considered a hopeless enterprise. My own marriage had been hastily arranged with little of my own participation; it was simply a matter of duty for me to take a wife and raise sons to carry on my father's blood and name. Now here they were, agonizing over Michael's lonely and helpless future and scheming to arrange a partner to provide eyes for him while he continued to depend on the mercy of strangers with this ridiculous notion of fee collection: *He was a beggar,* after all. Though

Michael had surpassed all my expectation of his limitations I had little hope for a pleasing union either for him or for his unfortunate bride. My own less-than-exciting marriage gave me little reason to congratulate Michael and Leah.

I have no explanation for Michael suddenly being able to see. Our mother was sure it was a miracle from heaven; Father refused to accept any explanation. People in the community were divided while the priests and rabbis would not even discuss the case except to deny any possibility of divine intervention. I had doubts but kept them to myself. Michael was always smart; he learned in months what it took me years to memorize in *bar mitsvah* preparation. He was blind but able to walk freely about the city while other blind beggars never moved from their posts. When he first confronted his fiancé after supposedly receiving his sight he wasn't even a little bit surprised to see she was a cripple and homely as a side of mutton. I don't claim that he could see all those years. But I can't help wondering.

Even more suspicious is the way Michael suddenly became a *melamed*, a teacher of boys. How did he learn to read so fast; where did he gain so much wisdom - and all the time being supported by his wife's father? It's just too neat and convenient. I'm not saying that Michael was a cheat… but still. What I do know is that I have worked for several decades slaughtering the beasts and carving their carcasses, as unlovely an occupation as the Master of the Universe has devised for his Chosen People, while my little blind brother has lived to enjoy the admiration and adulation of the whole community.

And his marriage! There is a surprise. Nothing in life seems to work out the way I expect. What, you think that a poor butcher is ill equipped to understand the workings of the world? Let me tell you: the study of Torah is the best education for life's preparation and I have continued my study until this very day. But nothing in Moses' writings prepared me for the reversals that came into our family when my brother married that homely crippled young woman. It was not just her affect on Michael; he was always a cheerful little tyke, even when I played tricks on him while he was learning to walk. He fell into the routine of married life like he had been preparing for it his whole life.

What Leah did to the atmosphere of my parent's home is something else. My father, the grumpish sour-faced butcher of cattle and carver of meats became a different person whenever Leah was near. He no longer retreated to his study after meals and though his great shaggy beard hid any trace of a smile I could see in his eyes a light that never shown in the shambles. She called him *Papa*. We never called my father anything but Father. When he came in from a day of slaughtering sheep she would greet him with a hug around his grizzled neck. The closest I ever got to my father was a handshake on the day of my *bar mitzvah*. And my mother, the bossy matron and commander of the kitchen! The joy that came to her with Michael's vision seemed to overflow into her relationship with Leah. I would hear them in the kitchen, chattering to each other about anything and everything. Leah had never been allowed into her own mother's kitchen so had no cooking experience. She would perch herself on a stool at the counter where my mother was working and watch every operation. Soon she was peeling the vegetables and helping with the preparations while Mother would explain things to her between bits of gossip from the neighborhood. In contrast my wife and my mother would never be found together in the kitchen. At our house my wife was like my mother, ruling over her kitchen, needing no help, wanting no company.

At the dinner table Leah would ask my father endless questions about his day, the cost and supply of meats from the countryside, how he learned the trade and wasn't it lucky he had a fine strong son like me to be his assistant and someday wouldn't Aaron be the finest butcher in Jerusalem! My father would grumble some inaudible reply around a mouthful of my mother's *matzos*. Leah was able to jolly him in a way astonishing to the rest of us. Once she said to him, "Papa, you don't fool me a bit! You are *proud* of your sons: Aaron so strong and handsome and Michael the perpetual student and soon-to-be teacher of boys." Father ducked his head over his plate and mumbled something I couldn't understand while Leah, leaning close to the old tyrant, laughed merrily while we looked on in awe-struck silence.

According to our traditions marriage is meant to enrich the companionship of two people while providing for procreation. *Halakhah*, the Jewish law, explains this and other fine points of connection between husband and wife, including the most intimate activity of all. There is a great deal to do with mutual respect and meeting each person's needs and so on. Based on my own experience of marriage I could not see how this might work with a young man only recently able to see, with no social experience on the one hand, and on the other hand a woman unable even to walk properly, and lacking any feature of desirability. I have slaughtered chickens with more meat on them than she had on her wasted legs and thin arms, or anywhere else as near as I could tell. On the contrary they were as happy together six days, six months and six years after their wedding, as any two creatures since the Garden.

So there is Michael's story. As you can see it cannot be understood without including Leah in the telling. I must admit I am surprised at how well it has turned out for two people who started life with so little promise. Do I reveal a sense of envy? I admit that I see their marriage through the haze of my own experience but greater than that is my regret that I have never used the years of my Torah study as Michael has been able to do. He works with boys every day, introducing them to the wisdom, beauty and poetry of the ancient writings while my daily routine is the pre-slaughter inspection of another cow, the quick slice of the animals throat, the bleeding of the carcass hung by its hind legs, the stripping-off of the hide, another inspection of the carcass for defects and the final carving of the various parts. So yes, during these days I think of Michael and his house of joy and his career as a teacher and I regret the drudgery of my own life.

Chapter 8

BETHANY

Bethany is only two miles from Jerusalem. When Lazarus, a popular local figure, died following a brief illness there was a large gathering of people at his burial services grieving his loss. His only family were two sisters who had loved him dearly and were devastated at his untimely death. But something unexpected happened.

An itinerant rabbi, a good friend of the Lazarus family, appeared a few days after Lazarus' internment, said a few words outside the tomb, and suddenly Lazarus appeared, quite alive and in full health. The celebration that followed was laced through with astonishment and joy, but also with doubt and suspicion.

The execution of the rabbi that followed a few days after the resurrection of Lazarus was justified by the Temple hierarchy on the argument that this rabbi, performing his miraculous feats outside the religious establishment – even on the Sabbath – was stirring up the people and undermining the authority of the priests and Pharisees. The Romans, according to this theory, would disenfranchise them, remove the Temple and take away the very nationhood of Israel. It is better, they argued, "that one man die for the people than that the whole nation perish."

The Lazarus family was enraged. Lazarus' sister Martha was especially outspoken on the subject. She railed against the priests and Pharisees, making public statements and accusations against them, challenging their motives and appearing on the steps of the Temple. "Hateful they are," she cried. "They have killed the Son of G-d!" The official response was sudden and harsh. Lazarus and his sisters were banished from worship, were condemned in society and eventually driven from their home in Bethany.

Chapter 9

THE SEARCH FOR LAZARUS

Bethany is a village not far from Jerusalem and it was in Bethany that the Galilean had performed the most celebrated "miracle" according to the whispers. It was also the least credible of all his rumored feats. It was, according to popular reports, the raising to life a man who had been dead for several days. The story was that a man by the name of Lazarus had died and was entombed when this prophet or teacher or whatever he was, came at the request of Lazarus' family and called the dead man from the tomb.

Unlike some of the other miracles that were accomplished without notoriety, this event was announced loudly and publicly by the relatives of Lazarus and perhaps by Lazarus himself. Many believed that a miracle had been done and became believers in, and followers of the Galilean. Others rejected the idea seeing a threat to the authority of the Pharisees, who in turn feared that a popular uprising of the people would bring on a new Roman pogrom. A few who still claimed allegiance to the miracle-man claimed that it was this reaction of the Pharisees that led eventually to the conviction and death of the Galilean. Michael decided to visit Bethany.

Taking the direct approach Michael sought out the home of Lazarus but was immediately met by a collective resistance in the village. At first Michael believed that people were trying to protect the family from the notoriety following the miracle of Lazarus. But it soon became apparent to Michael that the village people had chosen to deny the very existence of Lazarus or any credibility to the story of his life and death experience. The stories being repeated on the streets of Jerusalem were denied in Bethany. Michael had understood that Lazarus had two sisters, Martha and Mary. Now it seemed that neither Martha nor Mary, nor their brother Lazarus had ever lived in Bethany.

This community reaction might have sent Michael away from Bethany with the conclusion that the report of Lazarus being raised from the dead was mere myth, with one exception: the people Michael spoke to were too quick with their denials. No one, when questioned, had to stop and think if they knew of the Lazarus family. They immediately denied the existence of such a family and Michael could not help wondering what was being hidden and continued his search. Finally he met a young man willing to talk to him.

Yes, Liam knew Lazarus and his sisters since their childhood in Bethany. And yes, he had heard about the miracle of Lazarus. Was he a witness to the raising of Lazarus from the dead? No, but he heard about it from a young woman who knew the family and was sure that it was true. What happened? Why were they no longer in Bethany? They had to leave because Martha and Mary, in their rage, made a loud public accusation against the Pharisees, that they were guilty of killing a man from G-d. No one in the village was willing to support them and finally their fear of the Pharisees forced Lazarus and his sisters to move on. Where were they now? Liam did not know, or was unwilling to tell, not knowing who Michael was and who he was serving in his investigation. In fact he would say no more, nor was Michael able to find anyone else in Bethany willing to speak of Lazarus and the man from Galilee.

Michael reported this conspiracy of silence to Leah who suggested maybe it was best that Michael abandon his search for someone to share experiences with. But Michael was all the more intrigued.

The Temple hierarchy seemed to be afraid of these accounts of the miracles performed by a man they had sentenced to death, just as the priests of his local synagogue had rejected Michael's own report. He was all the more determined to find someone who could testify from his own experience; it was not good enough to hear these reports second hand. Michael kept remembering the Galilean's words on that second encounter. How could he believe such a statement from a man who apparently had no power to save himself from conviction and a death sentence? On the other hand Michael had been given the gift of sight, apparently by the man's power. Was Michael's experience one of a kind or was it one of several such G-d-like acts? According to whispers on the street the stranger from Galilee had blessed many people. Michael decided to continue his search.

❧

Chapter 10

THE UNCLEAN MADE CLEAN

There were ten of them. They had confronted the Galilean from a distance, begging to be cured. "Master, have mercy on us," they cried. Followers of the teacher admonished them to stand away and keep their place. But the Galilean recognized their faith and pronounced them clean and directed them to go, speak to no one, but show themselves to the priest.

They went quickly to the Temple where they presented themselves for the priest's inspection according to the law of the leper. They told the priest that they had been lepers but believed they were now clean. He inspected them thoroughly and declared them, indeed, to be clean.

One of the men who had been diseased, whose name was Avhrem, tried to report how the roving teacher from Galilee had cured them of the dreadful condition they had each suffered for most of their lives. But the priest interrupted him.

"You are clean and have always been clean," he said.

"No, you don't understand," Avhrem replied. "Until an hour ago we were lepers, 'put out of the camp,' according to the law. We were unclean and despised. Then this man…" But he was interrupted again.

"Stop talking nonsense. You are clean. Go and enjoy your lives."

"But the man…"

"I don't want to hear any more about it! Go now!"

51

The men who had been unclean left the Temple quickly, confused but unwilling to argue further with the priest; he might decide they were not clean after all! Out on the street and free of the hateful condition they discussed what they should do next. Certainly they would not rejoin the leper community. On the other hand they had no friends among normal society and most had not been close to family members for many years.

Avhrem said he intended to return to the man who had healed them. He would fall at the man's feet and worship him, for surely he was a man from G-d. But the others had different plans. Some wanted to reestablish contact with family, while others intended to begin at once to enjoy the good things of life that had been denied them for their adult years.

"But don't you think we owe a debt of gratitude to the man? And don't you think we should make known his power – for others who need healing?"

"No," they said! "We were told only to speak the priest." In this way they convinced themselves they had no further need of the healer, and no responsibility to preach the good news. Each went off to make his own new life.

Avhrem went in search of his healer. When he found him he threw himself at the man's feet, thanking him and declaring his undying devotion. The healer raised Avhrem to his feet and said, "Here is a grateful one; but where are the other nine?"

The case of the ten lepers was not well known. There were few witnesses to their healing other than the teacher's followers, who would write about this and similar events many years later. The ten who were made clean had dispersed and evidence of the healer's work disappeared with them. The priest who had declared them clean never spoke of the sudden, unprecedented healing of ten lepers. .

Chapter 11

AN INTERVIEW WITH LEPERS

One of the rumors about the Galilean and his storied accomplishments involved a group of lepers being cured. Some said there were 20 in the group, some said no, there were only six. But whatever the number, Michael was sure that if the report was true he would be able to find someone to give a first-hand report. The leper colony was large and, for social and hygienic reasons, separate but cohesive. If there had been a mass healing, it would be well known, perhaps even documented, in the leper community.

The lepers of Jerusalem were easy enough to find, having been separated from the "clean" citizens of the city. In defiance of the better judgment that dictated distance be maintained - the lepers signaling their presence by calling out "unclean, unclean" - Michael made his approach to a few lepers he found working at the city's burning dump yards. What could they tell Michael about the lepers who had been made clean? Where were they now? What were their names? At first, as Michael stood off at a discrete distance, the lepers ignored him, turning their backs in bitter contempt. Michael stepped closer and repeated his questions, offering an apology for his interruption of their work. Then, seeing their resentment he said,

"I understand you. I, too, was once cursed. I was born blind but a man appeared one day as I begged by the roadside. He touched me and now I see. We have heard that some of you had the same experience and I want to talk to them."

At these words one of the lepers stopped his searching among the rubbish, stood, turned slowly to Michael and said, "Those are pretty words, friend. But your miracle man did nothing for us. You can see with your new eyes, but where is the wonder in that? We see well enough, but look at us! We have been cursed; we are cursed; and we will be cursed until we die." Michael was stunned by these words and suddenly felt shame for his good condition compared to these wretched ones.

"Excuse me; I don't mean to boast of my good fortune. I merely want to understand what has happened to me, and as I have heard, to your friends."

"Our only friends are among us here in the refuse of the city. You good citizens of Jerusalem want nothing from us and we ask nothing from you except to be allowed to scavenge in your garbage. Since being struck down with this cursed condition we have been well aware of the purity of you who are clean. A few more with such good fortune – what is that to us?"

Michael persisted for a while but was met only with a stubborn resistance to his questions. It seemed that these outcasts had no interest in those who had been singled out from their midst, leaving them behind to continue in their hopeless lives. This was a new lesson for Michael. People see only their own situations in life, envying those better off, disregarding any moral certitude beyond their own misery. In any case, it was clear that Michael would learn nothing about lepers being made clean. Whether they were six or twenty, they may or may not have existed; they may or may not have been made clean. But these lepers, with their refusal to either confirm or to deny, suggested to Michael that in fact the same man who had changed his life had had a profound effect on some of these wretched few. The question was, why choose some for the miracle while leaving so many in their misery?

Leah listened carefully to Michael's report of his confrontation with the lepers. She, too, was puzzled at their refusal to speak of the rumored miracle, the healing of several from the local leper colony. She knew well of the despair that comes with a life-long crippling condition. But there was a conflict in her own mind: She was born a cripple into a wealthy family. She never lacked otherwise for the things that made life pleasant. And now she found herself in a joyful marriage she had never imagined for herself. How could she identify with those lepers, driven from society, doomed to scrabble among the city's dirt? Leah advised Michael to forgive them their bitterness. But she shared Michael's wonder for the purpose of all these miracles, if in fact, there were miracles in addition to his own.

Michael had not yet been able to authenticate reports of the Galilean's unlikely power. No one would speak to him about Lazarus, reportedly raised from the dead. The lepers refused to discuss those of their own number who were said to have been cured.

Michael would make one more attempt.

Chapter 12

JERICHO

Jericho is a town a day's walk from Jerusalem. Michael went there to interview another man reported to have received his sight at the hands of the Galilean. This man, too, had been a beggar it was said, and Michael believed they would have much in common - if the rumor were true. Finding the man proved to be difficult, however. With Jericho's history of invasion by the Hebrews after their many years as wanderers in the desert, the people of the city were disinclined to be impressed by modern miracles. According to the prophets Joshua had led those ancients to the city walls that crumbled before him. Joshua took possession of the city slaughtering every living resident – people and animals alike. The treasure of the city became the treasure of the Israelites and now, several centuries later, they lived proudly with their heritage. A beggar receiving his sight was not such a great event in the view of these immodest people.

Michael continued his search in the squares and marketplaces of the city. Finally he came across an elder of the community who suggested Michael talk to a man named Zacchaeus. "You want to talk about miracles? Here's a real miracle for you. Zacchaeus was a tax collector for the Romans and as everyone knows, there is no more despised creature among the Jews. They line their pockets by skimming from the taxes collected from their hard-working neighbors. Zacchaeus was worse than a leper! But can you believe, after a couple hours with this scruffy preacher (from Galilee of all places), Zacchaeus began giving away his money! First, according to people in a position to know, Zacchaeus gave half of all he owned to the poor, then began to go back over his records and where-ever he found that he had cheated someone, he repaid him – not in equal amount, can you believe it, but many times over! There is a real miracle for you!"

Zacchaeus was not hard to find in the city. Each time Michael mentioned the name "Zacchaeus" someone would grin broadly and tell more stories about the reformed tax collector. Eventually Michael found his way to the famous man's home where he was welcomed warmly. Michael explained his search for a blind beggar who had received his sight but before Michael could tell his story Zacchaeus began with a lively recitation of his own story about the "teacher".

"You have no idea," he said. "I didn't know anything about the guy except for wild stories involving people being cured of this or that affliction, but I heard he was coming through the city so out of curiosity I went to see what he might do here. But even before I could introduce myself he spoke my name as though he knew me and invited himself to my house! Incredible! There I was, a rich man with my hand in everybody else's pocket, and this Hebrew teacher who was said to be an incorruptible moralist walks boldly into my house. There were plenty of righteous Jews objecting to that, I can tell you! I couldn't stop laughing! What an afternoon we had; I never heard anyone talk like that one, telling lively anecdotes about his experiences, first as a reluctant carpenter's apprentice, later as a confident young scholar confounding his elders with his learning and logic. And didn't he make himself comfortable, eating my food, drinking my wine just as though he was one of the family! Not sure what came over me but I suddenly felt small and dirty because of my activities to that point, so even though the Teacher had made no criticism of my life or my habits, I began to vow to change. I heard myself promising to share what I had. More than that I said I would pay back what I owed to people I had cheated – over and above what I had taken! I kept thinking, 'I can't believe what I'm saying,' but I never felt so alive or so happy! And you know what? I did what I said I would do and am still doing it and I'm *still a rich man!!* How do you explain that?"

Michael, a man who was not wealthy, who still depended on his father-in-law for support, was impressed by Zaccheous' story but finally changed the subject to his own concern. He described his experience at the hands of the Galilean and explained his attempt to chase down some of the rumors of similar experiences. Were these real miracles or was there some other explanation?

Zaccheous responded that in his case, he saw it as a kind of miracle – he could never have believed there was anyone in the world able to make a generous man of him! On the other hand he also had to admit that his conversion was not nearly as dramatic as Michael's. There was a man, however, whose experience was similar to Michael's, a blind beggar who claimed the Teacher had restored his sight. That was the man Michael had come looking for! Where could he be found? Zaccheous and the beggar, whose name was Bartimaeus, would never have been friends in the old days. Bartimaeus, so full of praise and love for the Teacher had followed the man into Jericho as one of his devoted followers. In fact he was still in the city and was one of the few people still praising the memory of the Teacher in spite of the man's execution. Michael made an appointment to see Bartimaeus.

Chapter 13

BARTIMAEUS

Bartimaeus began to lose his sight when he was seven years old. His vision became progressively weaker until he was completely blind by the time he was twelve. He described the time to Michael thinking that the two men must have had similar experiences. Those years were a slow descent into darkness for him. From then and for the next 40 years he lived the bitter life of the helpless beggar. He received no education, as Michael had. Why should he have made an effort since G-d had condemned him to a useless existence? Instead he lived each day remembering the delights of his first seven years in the world. Why was he deprived of the beauty he recalled? He could feel the warmth of the sun but could no longer enjoy the color of the early evening sky. Boys and young men his age described the delights of falling in love; this girl or that woman was a beauty – you should see her, they said. It was very cruel!

Bartimaeus refused instruction and was unable even to recite the *haftarah* blessing at his bar mitzvah. In Bartimaeus' mind any study of the Torah was clearly forbidden to him since G-d obviously wanted him to be a life-long illiterate. *It was meant to be!* He settled into his beggar's calling satisfied that he was entitled to the support of strangers. He had nothing to contribute to society and he owed nothing to the institutions of G-d.

As Michael listened to Bartimaeus' history he began to realize that he and the other man had less in common than he had supposed. Yes, they had both been blind beggars, and yes they had both gained their sight. But Bartimaeus' blindness was far different from Michael's. During Michael's years of sightlessness he had no memory of, or appreciation for the scenes and images of the surrounding world. Michael did not suffer the bitterness of loss – he never knew what he had been deprived of until later when he gained his sight, whereas Bartimaeus could remember and mourn his loss. But the differences were even greater than that.

Bartimaeus looked closely at Michael, then began to speak from his heart.

"You are a young man," he said, "able to enjoy a whole lifetime as a normal human being, now no longer the life of a pitiful beggar. You can even read and write; I am doomed to illiteracy. You have a wife; I have never known the love of a woman, and never will. Your life of darkness was but a few years; mine was from my youth to this late age when I have few years left and little to look forward to.

"The day the Galilean came through here I had heard of some of his feats of magic and begged, like the beggar I was, for him to give me back my eyes. Without hesitation the man said to me, "Receive your sight. Your faith has healed you." I was astonished, of course, when I could suddenly see again. I wanted to wrap my arms around the man's feet and worship him. I followed him for several days, praising him and his work. But he's dead now and no one is being healed these days. Too bad I didn't meet him 30 years ago. "So what is your conclusion from your experience with the man," asked Michael. "I have met men who are bitter because someone other than themselves was healed. I have come across people who, I am sure, were witnesses to a most remarkable event yet they stubbornly refuse to speak of what they saw. You were healed but wish it had happened earlier in your life. I myself was healed yet I am confused by what it all means. What do you think?"

"I don't know what to think. I am not a learned man. As a child I could see, then spent the next 40 years in darkness, after which my sight was restored in time for me to die. What lesson can I learn from this? The man was said to be a descendant of David. He was expected to do great things for his people and he did - for a few of us. But the man is gone now and the Romans are still here; what have his people to show for his life? You explain it to me."

Chapter 14

THE VISITOR

One night, while Michael was conducting his search in Jericho, a visitor came to Leah's door. The visitor introduced herself as Esther and asked if Leah was the wife of the man who had mysteriously received his sight. Leah said that yes, she was. The woman then said she would like to speak to Leah about her husband's experience: How did it happen, what was the rabbi like who had performed this apparent miracle, and how did Leah's husband understand what had happened to him?

Leah replied that she had no first-hand information about the event and that Esther ought to speak to Michael when he returned from his trip.

No, Esther could not speak with Michael; she wanted only to learn from Leah whatever she could tell her. Finally Leah, recognizing the same curiosity in Esther that Michael was experiencing, invited the woman into the house. They would have tea and she would tell as much as she knew.

Over tea Leah told Esther what Michael had told her, that on the day he met the rabbi from Galilee there was very little conversation except between the rabbi and his friends. The rabbi put something on Michael's eyes and sent him to the pool of Siloam where Michael washed his eyes and received his sight. That's all there was to it and Michael had no other explanation. But why was Esther so interested in what had happened? Many people had approached Michael with these questions and his answers were always the same; his experience was well known by now.

Esther said that she was curious about these things because she, too, had had an encounter with the rabbi. In fact he had saved her life; he had actually *changed* her life.

"Tell me," Leah replied. "I would like to hear your story."

Esther was quiet for a few moments, then changed the subject.

"Is it true," she asked, "that when you and Michael first met he was still blind but that he received his sight before you were married?"

"Yes, that is all true."

"But didn't it change things for Michael, having his sight given to him just then?"

With a tight little smile Leah replied, "No, Michael has told me quite emphatically that his first sight of this homely face and my crippled condition did nothing to change his mind."

"I am so sorry! I didn't mean it that way! It's just that men, being as they are, might feel they prefer to experience life a little, being able to see for the first time, before being tied down in marriage."

"No, Michael and I were in love before he could see, were still in love later and are to this day very much in love."

"You are a lucky couple. It doesn't always work that way, has been my observation."

Leah leaned closer to the woman and looked directly into her eyes. "You didn't come here at this late hour of the night to ask about my marriage. What did the rabbi do for you that you are reluctant to talk about now?"

"Ah, Leah. You are much younger than I had expected, and very innocent. I am afraid that my life and my story would be shocking to you. Nor could you ever understand …"

"Try me."

"Well then…

"I compromised myself. You have always had a good and secure life with food and shelter and protection of a family who loved you. I could only gain those things for myself by giving myself …"

"I don't understand."

"No, of course not. You could never understand what it is like to have to sell yourself."

"I still don't understand. Sell yourself, how?"

"Leah, Leah… Don't you see? Men came to me and I *gave them what they wanted*. There are many fine, upstanding men in this community I was able to make happy for a few hours."

"You mean … I don't believe it! You were a prostitute?"

"Now you mustn't cry, or I will too and I have long since given up feeling sorry for myself."

"But that is just horrid!"

"Yes. It is the abomination for which I was condemned to death by the Sanhedrin. And perhaps I deserved it."

"What happened?"

"I was brought into the public square and stood up before a circle of teachers of the Law and Pharisees. There were little piles of stones already arranged around the circle and everything was prepared for my execution. They turned to this young rabbi who had been teaching in the Temple courts and addressed him first with respect. 'Teacher,' they said. 'This woman was caught in adultery. According to the Law of Moses she should be stoned. What do you have to say about that?'

"Now I never paid much attention to Moses' Law or the traditional practices of our people but I have done some research since and find a miscarriage of justice in my case. In the first place I was not caught in adultery; it was malicious gossip that brought me to the noble Pharisees. In the second place Moses told us that when a man commits adultery with another man's wife both the adulterer and the adulteress are to be put to death. He doesn't say anything about stoning. Stoning is reserved for other abominations, such as sacrificing one's children to Molech."

"So they were going to stone you. Were they also going to stone the men you had been with?"

"Oh, no. That's the injustice of the thing. I alone was to be stoned. In a kind of twisted logic, apparently because I was not another man's wife, it was not a case of classic adultery! My accusers seemed to overlook the fact that adultery requires the activity of more than one person.

"Perhaps I temporize. Whether stoning was the justifiable punishment, or whether a lack of a husband for me protected my 'clients,' I suppose I was guilty none the less. But there is one other aspect to this business – a little matter of due process, as the lawyers like to say. There is a proverb: 'The first to present his case seems right, till another comes forward and questions him.'"

"You have a knowledge of judicial procedure. How were your arguments dealt with by your accusers?"

"Leah, my innocent friend. Don't you see, I had no knowledge of the Law then and I had no standing to argue before the Pharisees. Nor did I have an advocate to present my case. But on reflection I can see now that this whole sorry business was not about me. It was all about that young rabbi who was attracting so much attention among the people with his radical teachings and his independence from the hierarchy of the Temple."

"And so what happened? Your splendid beauty and good health suggest to me that you escaped the stoning."

"When they asked the rabbi his opinion, I hoped that perhaps he would have a word in my defense, though why he should I had no idea. Instead he seemed to give his assent to the stoning. He said to let the one without sin cast the first stone. I cringed and wrapped my arms around my head. I could see that the supply of stones, each the size to just fit in a man's hand, was meant to kill but not all at once. It would take an accumulation of blows, no one of which could be said to be the fatal stone, sparing any one man from the thought that he was the executioner. So careful are the planners of an execution to spare the executioners from an inconvenient sense of guilt!"

"But you said that the rabbi saved you."

"I waited for the first blow which never came. I looked up and saw first one then another of the older men in the crowd begin to walk away. They were followed by more until no one was left in the square but the rabbi and me. He was crouched down and seemed to have been writing something in the dirt with his finger. I leaned over trying to see what he was writing. It looked like some kind of list – perhaps a list of names. (I like to think that they were the names of some of my clients!) Then he stood up and asked me where everybody was – had no one condemned me? He said that he would not condemn me either, but that I should go and lead a clean life.

"Now it is late. I am exhausted and you must be too so I will leave. But perhaps you will allow me to come again to talk over tea in your warm, wonderful home."

Several days later Leah and Esther were having tea in Leah's garden. Esther said, "Leah, my sweet friend. You are the only person I can talk to. No one else will have anything to do with a whore and no one will believe that a whore can be reformed. Once a whore always a whore, they say.'"

"Esther, *my beautiful friend*, you mustn't talk that way. You are a decent person who has had a terrible life. You were afraid I would be shocked by your story. Instead I have been educated. And what an education! You must meet Michael; you and he have so much you could discuss about the rabbi."

"No, I know you cannot understand this. But for ten years I practiced every method to attract men to myself. I cannot pretend now to be able to speak to another woman's husband in innocence. It is enough for me to open my heart to you. I have learned from you something I never could have believed, that it is possible for a man and a woman to have a love that only gives and asks nothing in return except for more love. I can see that you love your Michael very much."

"I do love him. And I love his big nobbly feet. And his strong legs that are like great pillars of strength next to my spindly sticks."

"You are so good. I only hope my story will not turn your gentle view of life into cynicism. Your husband would not thank me for that."

"You need have no fear on that account. My husband has his own view of the religious establishment. I will tell you a secret about my husband. But you must never repeat it to anyone! It is something known only to Michael's family."

"I will carry your secret to the grave along with my gratitude for your trust."

"When Michael's mother discovered he was blind, only a few minutes after his birth, she became so much in despair and so enraged at a G–d who would allow such a thing to happen without reason that she sent the *mohel* away forbidding the circumcision. Nor did she ever relent, even in the face of the furious insistence of her husband and the rabbi!

"It amused Michael to point out to me on our wedding night that I had apparently married an infidel."

"You have taken me into your confidence," Esther said. "I will share with you my opinion of our people and their prejudices.

"Why do you suppose women must be separated from men, even in the worship services of the synagogue? And our hair: Why must it be covered or shorn, as though we were flaunting our own glory? And G-d forbid that a woman's arms should be bare! Why all these strange attitudes? I will tell you why. It is because of the weakness of men! *They must be protected from their own lust!* Ever since that strumpet Eve led her silly husband astray we have been blamed. But it's not *our* fault; it is *their* fault! It is their own weakness but we have carried the blame ever since the Garden. If it wasn't for woman, man could be sin-free! Am I bitter? Yes, of course I am bitter. I have seen men at their worst, when they have lost all restraint in their rutting. They used me then despised me and finally I should be stoned in the public square. In my opinion circumcision doesn't go far enough. It should be taken to a logical extreme then we could *all* enjoy a sin-free life!" Leah commented dryly that that could spell the end of the whole Jewish race. The two women smiled, each with her own thoughts as they continued drinking their tea.

Chapter 15

THE INNKEEPER

Returning to Jerusalem from Jericho Michael found a small country inn by the side of the road. While staying there he raised the issue of the healings: did the innkeeper know of any healings in this neighborhood, similar to those reported in the Jerusalem area? The innkeeper only shrugged, acknowledging reports and rumors, but for him there was no first-hand experience of such unlikely occurrences. People were inclined to be excited by the possibility of magical events, and all such reports should be ignored as the wishful thinking of superstitious fools. For instance there was the time one man was supposed to have fed several thousand people from a small basket of food. Absurd! Michael decided not to speak of his own experience but brought up the issue of the apparent miracle-worker. In the reports and rumors the innkeeper had heard, was there ever a description of the man performing the "miracles"? Oh sure; in almost every instance there appeared to have been one charismatic character responsible for the "miracle". The man was variously described as a young rabbi, an earnest teacher, a radical philosopher or a slightly mad modern Ezekiel. Michael sorted through these descriptions, trying to find a similarity to the Galilean of his experience.

After a few moments, while both men pondered the question of miracles, those inclined to believe in them, and the one supposed to have performed them, the innkeeper made a surprising statement. Though he was skeptical of the miracles of healing, he believed that he had actually met the man described as the healer. Michael asked for a description and the innkeeper, since it was a quiet evening with Michael as his only guest, and because he enjoyed the role of storyteller, folded his hands over his large belly and told the following.

"A few years ago, on a night much like this with not many travelers on the road, a small group of men appeared at the door to my inn. There were five men in the group, led by one large burly chap who negotiated for room and board for the night for the group, directed his companions to where they should stow their belongings, and went with my son to the shed out back to arrange care for the group's two donkeys. This fellow was a tall, powerful-looking character, with a thick white beard, a strong voice and imperious manner, and was surely the leader of the group. I studied him carefully and seeing the man's huge hands, scarred and callused, I decided he must be a laborer – perhaps a farmer or fisherman.

"After finishing the evening meal the group made themselves comfortable in front of an open fire in the common room of my inn. I joined them after finishing the kitchen chores and soon discovered that the big fisherman was not the real leader of the group. At first he held forth on the subject of their travels and the next destination, speculating as to the reception they might receive in Jerusalem; he did not seem optimistic of a warm welcome, for some reason. As he began to complain about the stiff-necked Temple leaders, another one of the men started to speak. This one was younger – perhaps twenty-five years old or so – and had the speech of a learned man, like a scholar or a rabbi. The big fisherman immediately stopped talking and focused his whole attention on the speaker, as did the others in the group. I was interested to hear what this one had to say but was not immediately impressed.

"The young rabbi began to talk about the respect we should have for our leaders; their lives are as difficult as ours while they carry the additional burden of a moral responsibility for the people. We should respect and support them, with the same love and compassion we have for all men. He went on at length in that vein with a theory of social ethics I found to be charming but altogether unrealistic."

Michael interrupted and asked, "Did he seem to be a teacher or was he some kind of home-grown philosopher?"

"It seemed to me that he was probably a rabbi as I said before, so he was a teacher by definition. But his teaching was altogether new to me, with lots of blather about love for our fellow man and such wishful thinking. In fact I began to be a little put out since it seemed the man was preaching to *me*. Perhaps I was being overly sensitive, but as an innkeeper I have learned not to place too much respect and trust in my fellow man. This fairytale idea that we ought to treat every stranger with the same compassion we feel for our own family members – in fact for ourselves as well – I found to be the suggestion of someone with very little experience in the real world."

"Go on. I find all this to be quite fascinating."

"Well, okay for you, but after listening to this stuff for a while I could stand it no more and offered my own thoughts. Had the rabbi known *even one man* in the whole world able to live according to these ethical standards? The rabbi studied me intensely then, in a reversal asked a question that seemed to be a challenge to me in response to my challenge to him. Had *I* not seen such a man, myself?

"This surprised me and reminded me of a strange experience I had had many years before. Somewhat sheepishly I admitted that I had, sort of. Would he like to hear the story? The rabbi settled back in his chair, and with a smile said yes, he would very much like to hear my story. His companions seemed a little annoyed that I had interrupted the man's discourse, but they, too, settled back for the telling."

Michael spoke up at this point. "I want very much to hear your story and will also settle back for the telling."

The innkeeper was clearly pleased with himself and flattered to have such an attentive audience, so after pouring himself another glass of the local wine, he settled back for the telling.

"I will relate the story exactly as I told it to them that night.

"It happened some years prior to the night of the rabbi and the fisherman.

"A traveling businessman spent a night in my inn, roused himself early the next morning and prepared to set out on the road for Jericho where he said he had commercial interests. I warned him about traveling on this road after sundown. Robbers and thieves made it dangerous especially for people traveling alone. He said he understood, and that was why he was determined to get an early start. He believed he could reach Jericho easily in eight hours. He left, walking with his loaded donkey and I thought no more about him. But at about noontime I looked out and saw him returning, leading his donkey with a rider slumped over on the animal's back, hugging the neck of the beast like a drunken lover.

"I went out to meet him, thinking he had met an injured acquaintance. He said no, the man was a stranger he found nearly dead, in a ditch by the side of the road. He had apparently been attacked by thieves. I was astonished because, as you know, one does not assume a responsibility for strangers. Who knows where such a burden may lead, and for what? Then I began to suspect that the businessman had recognized the stranger as some important person; assisting him could be good for business. I helped carry the man into a room in the inn where the businessman stripped the torn and bloodied clothes from the stranger and began to clean him and bathe his wounds. The man was barely conscious, having suffered an ugly bruise to the side of his head. It seemed unlikely to me that he would live, but I could see the advantage to the businessman when he reported to the man's grateful family all he had tried to do for him. I left them alone in the room thinking I would get the whole story after the man had finally expired. But an hour later the businessman came down to the kitchen for a cup of soup, which he intended to feed to the poor fellow. He was alive and conscious but terribly weak from his ordeal, he told me.

"Some time later the businessman joined me in the lounge and I had an opportunity to ask some questions, discreetly at first, not wanting to probe too deeply into the man's motives. "So tell me," I said. "How did you find this fellow?"

"'I found him lying face down in a watery ditch, next to the road,' he said. 'Just as you warned me, robbers had attacked him, beating him mercilessly, and leaving him to die. When I found him there was nothing of value left to him, nor was there so much as a scrap of paper to identify him.' How clever to imply he did not know the identity of the stranger, I thought to myself.

"'Would you believe,' he continued, 'the fellow was lying there in that ditch in plain sight to anyone passing by. And there were many travelers on the road this morning; dozens must have seen him there and walked on by. How heartless people can be!'

"Now I was beginning to wonder about my theory. 'Do you really mean to say that you stopped there, out of a sense of reckless generosity to help the fellow, without knowing who he was?'"

"'Of course I did not know who he was! He was half submerged in ditch water and covered with mud and blood. How could I know who he was? I still don't know who he is.'

"'Excuse me, but if that is the case, do you realize what you have done? Now you are responsible for the man. What if he died - to whom would you report his death? And even worse, now that he lives, how will you care for him? Surely you don't intend for me to assume the burden. Nursing him back to health will be a costly enterprise and this inn is no hospital.'

"He looked at me with a kindly expression, and answered patiently. 'Relax; I don't expect you to assume my responsibility. I will leave tomorrow morning to continue on my business but I will leave money to pay for the man's bed and board and whatever medicine he may need until he is well enough to travel. I will come this way again in about ten days to check on him and if you need more money I will pay you then.'

"I was astonished at this highly unlikely attitude. I have been innkeeper to hundreds of travelers going through this place; I have heard their tales and have listened to their stories of the road. Men have been robbed and cheated, lied to and betrayed. Once in a while a stranger may lend a hand to another, if the cost in time is not too great and no money is involved. But never have I heard of such reckless generosity as shown by this one – and a businessman at that!

"As he mounted his donkey in the morning he handed me a bag of coins more than enough to keep the patient until his recovery. 'I'll be back in ten days. If you need more at that time I will pay you. And thank you,' he said to me, as though it was my kindness that was providing for the man.

"But the injured man was gone before ten days had passed. He had been so well cared for that he was walking the second day, eating like a healthy horse the third day and making tentative forays beyond my inn on the fifth day. On the morning of the seventh day he ate a hearty breakfast and announced that he was feeling fine and would be on his way. I suggested that his benefactor would return in three days and wouldn't he like to stay and thank him for all he had done for him?"

"'I think not,' he said. 'I have been gone too long from my family. I am going home.'

"He gathered his few belongings, claimed the remaining coins left by the businessman for his care, and set off on the road to Jerusalem. At the last moment he called back to me over his shoulder, 'When that fellow returns say 'thanks' to him for me.'"

Michael thought for a few moments, then said, "It is an amazing story. How was it received by the rabbi and his friends?"

"Wait, I haven't told you the best part! On the tenth day the traveling businessman returned, just as he said he would. I was expecting him to be disappointed and perhaps angry that the fellow went off the way he did, with so little gratitude for the generous assistance, but no. He expressed only pleasure and satisfaction at the quick recovery and made some lame joke about his own medical expertise.

"'Aren't you curious to know who he was or where he was headed when he left here?' I asked. The businessman replied that he did not need to know any more about the fellow than that he recovered and was well.

"Once again I was surprised by this fellow's unlikely attitude but the biggest surprise was yet to come."

"Please tell me," said Michael as the innkeeper sank further into the cushions of his chair, and took another long swallow of wine.

"It was like this and you will probably not believe it: As the man was climbing onto his donkey and about to ride happily out of my life, I realized I knew nothing about him. I said to him, 'If you are going home, where is home?'"

"He said, 'My home is Samaria.'

"'Samaria,' I said! 'You are telling me that you are a Samaritan?' The fellow looked at me with a knowing smile. He could see that as a pious Jew, not only would I look down my long aristocratic nose at him, I would naturally doubt the possibility of a lowly Samaritan doing what he had done for a stranger."

"It seems unlikely that a Samaritan would find much success doing business in Jerusalem and Jericho," observed Michael.

"You know nothing of the realities of commerce in the city. A man might cross the street to avoid the unpleasantness of meeting a despised Samaritan but if there's an opportunity to make a shekel or two doing business with him … well, okay."

"And the rabbi's response to your tale?"

"He had no response except to say, 'That was a good man and a good story. I will remember it' With his companions, however, it was different. The big fisherman had a look of doubt and distaste on his face. Either he didn't believe my story or else he was disturbed at the idea of a Samaritan in such a role. One of the other men merely kept his eyes down, as though looking for an explanation at his feet. The other two were clearly puzzled and looked quickly to the rabbi for his reaction.

"After a few moments the rabbi began to speak. 'You have all judged the man on the basis of his heritage. Because of your warped bias about Samaritans you believe one could not have shown compassion for a stranger, so you doubt the story. But the real issue is, what would *you* have done in that situation? Would you have stopped to help or would you, too, have walked on by. And is that why you are disturbed, because of the suggestion that a lowly Samaritan is capable of more love for his fellow man than you yourselves are?'

"The men took this rebuke without meeting the rabbi's eyes, nor would any of them debate the point or protest their own willingness to help in such a situation.

"The rabbi continued his lesson in social ethics. 'We live in a small world,' he said. 'Life in this world would be better if we treated every man as a neighbor rather than as a stranger.'"

Michael noticed a change in the innkeeper's tone as he was concluding this account. There was an expression in his voice, as though, finally, even he was moved by the rabbi's words.

"Finally, then, what is your conclusion from all this mystery" asked Michael. "Is the rabbi's philosophy of life realistic or is it a dream? Can men actually treat each other with love, in the rabbi's words, or are we too selfish? And by the way, who was this 'rabbi'? Was he the miracle-worker we have heard so much about or was he merely a teacher with a radical message?"

The innkeeper was deep in thought, perhaps remembering the atmosphere of those moments with the rabbi. Then he seemed to wake from his reverie. "I have already told you: I can't believe in a miracle that happened to someone else. I'll believe when one happens to me! As for the mysterious rabbi I have no explanation for the feeling in this room as he was speaking, nor do I wish for him to return to my inn; I could never run a successful establishment applying the rules for living that he preached.

"In any case I think that my story proved my point. In spite of the rabbi's teaching of good works, and in spite of all the reckless Samaritan businessman did for the stranger, what was there to show for it all? That ungrateful stranger accepted the kindness and assistance that saved his life and went off with a mere 'thanks" as an afterthought. I didn't notice any difference in the world the next day, nor have I seen a change in the way men treat each other ever since. And if that rabbi was actually the 'miracle worker' we hear so much about where is he now, can you tell me?"

Michael despaired of changing the outlook of the cynical innkeeper and kept his thoughts and his own remarkable experience to himself. But he believed that his Galilean benefactor was the rabbi of the story and was more eager than ever to discover more about the man and his life. One thing the innkeeper had said was of interest to Michael: the reference to feeding several thousand people; this was news to him. He decided to research the incident.

Chapter 16

THE FEEDING

A small group of men, followers of a teacher/prophet who had gained a reputation for doing good, set out on their own pilgrimage to spread a message of reconciliation and repentance. Like their mentor they brought healing to many people during their journeys about the countryside. Finally, exhausted, they reported back to the teacher on their progress. They hoped to enjoy a sort of retreat in some quiet place where they might rest.

But news of their activities had spread through the surrounding towns and villages, and people in large numbers began to follow them everywhere. When word got out that the men and their leader intended to camp in a certain place, large crowds began to gather there in anticipation. When the teacher arrived with his followers he was confronted by all these people eagerly awaiting him; hoping to hear from him; like sheep without a shepherd. So he spoke to them at length about the kingdom of G-d until late in the afternoon when his followers urged him to conclude his remarks so that the people could go into the neighborhood to find something to eat. But the teacher had something else in mind.

"You feed them," he said. But his followers pointed out, quite reasonably, that they had no supplies of food adequate to feed such a large mob, which by then was numbered in the thousands. Taking the meager bits of food

they were able to gather he blessed the scraps and instructed them to make a fair distribution among the people. As it turned out, there was plenty for everyone; no one went away hungry and in fact there were basketfuls of leftover remnants.

Chapter 17

THE PICNIC

Michael set out for the region where the "feeding" was supposed to have occurred. He was sure that if there was any truth to the story, with so many people involved he would easily find some who could describe what happened that day. He had discovered that one way to gather local information, anecdote and rumor was in the inns and pubs of a village. He tried this tactic again with only a little success at first. Everyone he met who would talk about the incident could only speak from second hand observation; none had actually been present when it happened, but at least Michael had reason to believe there was something to the story. Then one afternoon a man in a pub mentioned that his wife had been in the crowd; perhaps Michael would like to talk to her? Michael would be grateful for an introduction. The woman was happy to talk about that day, but as it happened she was standing near the back of the large crowd of people who had gathered to hear the man speak and was not sure what, exactly had happened. The man was said to have a new message that would bring peace to the world and there was excitement among the people, many of whom had walked a great distance to hear him and she was unable to get close to him.

The woman wasn't much interested in his message, though; what she was hoping for was to see him perform some miraculous feat similar to what she had heard about.

"There was the time when some men brought a crippled friend to one of the preacher's meetings," she said. "The crowd was so big, they had to cut a hole in the building to get access to the speaker who, when he saw how determined the men were, cured the fellow right there on the spot!

"Then there was a wedding we heard about, where the preacher somehow provided all the food and wine and entertainment for the guests. *That's* the kind of thing I wanted to see. I expected that with so large an audience the man would do something really spectacular."

She continued, "My favorite is the one about the wild man who lived among pigs, a man no one could approach or talk to. It is said that this preacher ministered to the crazy man and made him sane while the pigs went crazy! That was the kind of performance I was hoping to see that day."

"But all he did was talk, talk, talk. I looked around in the crowd hoping to see someone ill or crippled who the man might cure before our very eyes. But this bunch of people all seemed to be sound in mind and body. Not a club foot or nut case anywhere in sight!"

Yes, Michael had heard quite a bit about the man's apparent miracles. What could she tell him about the meal that was supposedly served?

"Ah," she said. "That *was* a surprise. I never expected to be fed but as the day grew long we began to feel hungry. I'm not sure what happened but at one point the man stopped speaking when one of his assistants whispered something in his ear. I could not see very well what was going on but there was some fussing about in the front row with sounds of laughter and cheering. Suddenly large wicker baskets were being carried through the crowd by more of the man's assistants. I was certain there would be nothing left of whatever it was in the baskets by the time one of them reached me; I could see people helping themselves eagerly to bread and some kind of meat. But, indeed, soon a basket was held out to me and not only was it not empty; it was full of freshly baked bread and plenty of roasted fish that must have been caught that morning. I cannot tell you where all that food came from at the last moment on a warm afternoon; all I can say is that it was as fine a picnic as I have every enjoyed!

"By the way, I was told that there was as much food left in the baskets at the end of the picnic as at the beginning! I find that to be a bit much, don't you? An unnecessary exaggeration about a pleasant day."

"But," Michael replied, "Wasn't that similar to the wedding incident, where the man suddenly provided for the people? And didn't you consider his message of peace important, also – as another kind of feeding for the people?"

"Okay, okay; the world would be a better place if we just loved each other. But the idea that I can make peace with someone who hates me by letting him hit me again and again goes against all my instincts. Nor can I see anything blessed about being poor or in sorrow.

"Maybe the supply of fish and bread *was* similar to the wedding surprise but I missed the best part. I eventually saw the food and had some of it to eat, so I know it was real. But I didn't actually see him produce it out of thin air, so I don't know if it was a miracle or a trick. That part was quite disappointing in fact."

It was time for Michael to return home to Leah and recount his experiences with reluctant witnesses .

Chapter 18

Leah's Eyes

"Leah, my dear, when I gained my sight I thought that the most wonderful thing in the world was the written word and being able to read! But I have found that reading the page is nothing compared to reading people, and people are the most interesting books. How they love to talk, and tell their stories! I think that sometimes, while they are speaking they discover for themselves how they actually feel, and what they really believe. All I have to do is ask an occasional question, then listen quietly. I met a man, an innkeeper, who told me the most amazing story – and believe it or not it was a story inside a story with two surprise endings!"

Michael went on to tell of his stay at the inn, the innkeeper's tale about the injured traveler and the Samaritan, which he had told to the rabbi, whom Michael believed to be the Galilean, and the rabbi's reaction to the story, followed by the rabbi's stern lesson delivered to his friends. "The innkeeper professed not to believe in miracles unless one happened to him, but he was obviously impressed by the rabbi's message which he found to be challenging but too impractical for him to apply to his own life. Best of all was his account of one man's mercy and love shown to a stranger as though that man were his neighbor. See? The innkeeper offered his own example of the social ethics preached by the rabbi, then seemed to reject the principle. The lesson was as clear and beautiful as one of your wall hangings, but the innkeeper couldn't see it. Except that for just a moment or two he seemed to be lost in his own thoughts as he remembered the rabbi's words. I believe he was actually moved in his heart, but he quickly recovered to his cynical self.

"And the rabbi? It appeared to me the rabbi knew the innkeeper's story before he heard it.

"You taught me to read people's faces and the way they hold their hands when they speak. I have met people these last weeks who sometimes speak that language with more truth than with their words. The innkeeper said he didn't want to see the rabbi again but for a moment his eyes told me that he longed for such warmth in his own life.

"Then there was the woman and a 'picnic'.

"Ah, that one. She was the most disappointing of all my interviews. Several thousand people fed with apparently no preparation of food and all she cared about was the magic show she *didn't* see. She was even disappointed at the absence of the lame and the halt. Here was a man who held thousands spellbound for the better part of a day, and she was bored by his words.

"The most interesting part of my trip, however, was the bit about the rabbi and his rebuke to his followers and their reaction to the generosity of the Samaritan. I have to admit to some doubts in my own mind; since childhood I have heard of the lowly Samaritans and their undependable nature. When the Assyrians carried our people away 700 years ago, the ones the Assyrians considered not worth the trouble were the people of Samaria. So when our ancestors returned to Jerusalem they refused the help of the remnant Samaritans in rebuilding the Temple. This, I have always understood, was proof that the Samaritans are not real Jews and are not to be trusted.

"But the rabbi turned it all around and showed us, his followers, the innkeeper and even me – that our real reaction was due to a weakness in our own characters. We didn't want to believe a Samaritan (or anyone else) could show a generosity of which we ourselves were incapable. His followers were ashamed and even though I was not there for the rebuke I felt shamed as well, when I heard what he had said."

Leah a made her own critique of the innkeeper's tale. "In the first place 700 years is a long time to carry a grudge against a whole race of people. In the second place I think you give your innkeeper too much credit. From your description of him, he was a real shlump."

"A shlump? I don't know what a shlump is."

"You think he was moved by the rabbi's words but I suspect quite the opposite. I think he is a man so involved with his circumstances and his own life, he cannot find a generous spirit in himself. He was in the presence of someone quite special, and if we are right, and the rabbi of the story was the same man who gave you your sight … well, your innkeeper is a shlump compared to the tax collector who almost instantly recognized the greatness of the 'teacher' as he called him, and changed his life dramatically and voluntarily.

"Perhaps you are too good, my Michael, to see the failings in the people you meet. You must be careful in your evaluation of your fellow man."

"Ah my sweet wife, when your eyebrows come together like that I know I am about to learn a new lesson! How thankful I am for your insight that is keener than my eyesight."

Chapter 19

MICHAEL AND LEAH

Leah was worried about Michael's travels at first. She felt that from his years of blindness he had little preparation for the dangers of the open road. How would he find his way? Would he be too trusting of strangers? Did he realize that the generous people who had put coins in his cup all those years were not the same people he would meet on the road? She had warned him about the dangers of solitary travel though she herself had no such experience.

As always Michael respected his wife's wisdom and listened closely to her advice. By so doing, he had learned many lessons about people's dealings with one another. He found that he was sometimes too trusting, even naïve. So when he first started out on his search for the truth about the Galilean he was careful about joining other travelers on the road, but eventually found security in numbers when walking through the remote countryside. He discovered that he enjoyed the experience, seeing new places and meeting new companions.

In fact, Michael's "quest for the truth," as he called it, soon became the "thrill of the open road" in his mind. He regretted that Leah was unable to join him on these jaunts through the Judean countryside so each evening he filed away in his memory the events of the day to share later with his wife.

Michael was filled with wonder at the sights and sounds that had suddenly expanded from his small world of blindness into the infinite views from the ground at his feet to the limitless horizon.

It was not in Michael's character to be bitter like Bartimaeus about his lost years during that first quarter century of his life. He was only grateful for the new experience of freedom to take in the wonders around him. Some of the greatest wonders, he discovered, were associated with the people he met, their opinions and attitudes and their ways of interpreting life's unexpected twists and turns. He began to understand that different people had reacted differently to the events of their lives. One, like the blind beggar Bartimaeus who received his sight late in life, might be grateful at first but bitter later at the thought of his many years of blindness. Another, like the tax collector Lazarus, could be joyful and grateful to have been made aware of his own venality, to lead a life of generosity towards his fellow man. Each had experienced a miracle at the hands of the Galilean; each had reacted quite differently from the other.

For Michael every new encounter gave him new questions about human nature. And human nature soon became of greater wonder to him than the natural wonders he discovered with his new eyes. The silhouette of olive trees against the setting sun was one of his greatest joys in those first days. But such sights soon gave way to his wonder at the mysteries of the human spirit, and the surprise each new encounter added to his views about people. Leah was right: if he watched people closely as they talked, and if he listened carefully to their words, he might learn what was in their hearts. But he might also be confused by the apparent contradiction between what he could see and what he heard.

As the years passed Michael improved his reading and understanding of history and the traditions of his people; he became a *melamed*, a good teacher of language and social studies to young boys and his stature in the community grew. In the early years of their marriage Leah feared that as Michael progressed his need for her would fade; he would grow but she would stay as she was, a crippled wife. She feared that she would become more burden than companion to Michael. But Michael's years of blindness left him with a weakness he was never able to overcome. He seemed to have suffered an arrested development in his ability to understand reality by what he could see; he continued to rely too much on what he heard and sometimes doubted the evidence of his eyes in his dealings with people. He could be confused by the contradictions he encountered when what he heard people say was inconsistent with what he saw in their lives. This weakness left Michael with a naivete about people that could be a source of confusion and disillusionment for him. Leah supplied an understanding that Michael relied on for the remainder of their life together; their companionship only grew stronger as the years passed.

No confusion existed in Leah's mind regarding the marvel of their marriage. To Leah it seemed that the miracle of Michael's sight was no more remarkable than the miracle that changed her own life. She remembered the hopelessness of her early years, when she had reconciled herself to the life of the handicapped girl with no future beyond her weaving. There followed a succession of improbable events: First they were brought together in an unlikely matchmaking exercise. Next, Leah and Michael accepted each other in their early meetings. Then Michael received his sight making it unlikely they would continue their relationship, but Michael discovered that he could love the crippled and homely Leah when he could see her even more than when he could only hear her voice.

"So, my husband, you have trekked the countryside in your search for the truth. What is the truth of the matter, do you think"

"Perhaps the truth depends on what we believe it to be. Do we believe in a G-d, the Master of the Universe responsible for all there is and all there ever will be?"

"Of course we do."

"And do we believe he has touched our lives – yours and mine?"

"You know that we do.

"What of my eyesight: Was it given to me in a deliberate act of G-d, by the power of the Galilean?"

"It is the only explanation."

"If that is the case can we conclude that the Galilean was from G-d?"

"We must."

"Then what was the meaning of his life, and especially of his death?"

"I keep thinking of what the blind man of Jericho said. He quoted the Galilean as saying something about faith in connection with his healing," Leah replied.

"According to what Bartimaeus told me, the Galilean said, 'Receive your sight. Your faith has healed you.'"

"What do you suppose he meant? Can that be the key – simply a matter of belief?"

"It's a good theory, but in my case there was no faith involved. I was an empty vessel, standing by the road with my tin cup, with no other thought than the next clink of a coin."

"Yes, but what was it he said to his companions, when he was talking about the cause of your blindness?"

"He said, 'This happened so that the work of G-d might be displayed in his life.' I remember thinking those words were small comfort to me."

"It does seem strange that he should burst into your life like that, with no explanation except to make a philosophical point to his companions. Are we missing something?"

"There is something else I haven't told you; something I have never told anyone. Now it begins to make a little more sense to me; at the time I was merely mystified . . . the Galilean came back to me a few days after I received my sight."

Leah was astonished. "What? *What?* Why have you kept this from me!? What happened? What did he say? Tell me – you must! I am your wife and we will have no secrets!"

"Calm down and stop pulling my beard! Where is the gentle weaver I married? Now she is a tiger, ready to cross-examine me like a true Pharisee!"

Michael continued, "It was after I got thrown out of the synagogue. He came looking for me and found me at a time when I was really down."

"What did he say to you?"

"He wanted to know if I believed in 'the son of man'. I had no idea what he meant by this expression, and told him so. I said that if I knew him I could believe in him. He said I was speaking to him. It was all very strange to me, but I was prepared to take seriously anything he told me and I can say without embarrassment that at that moment I truly loved the man."

"But what did it all mean? Was he trying to explain something, referring to himself as 'the son of man'? I have never heard the expression."

"It took me a while to make sense of it, but I did some research and asked some questions of an old rabbi who had taught me when I was still a blind boy. (He's one of the few rabbis willing to have anything to do with me now.)

"He sent me to the writings of Daniel most of which is a mystery to me, having to do with strange prophesies with images of beasts with horns and iron teeth and rivers of fire and so on. It didn't help that I was still learning to read and it was pretty slow going for me. But then I came across those words, 'son of man.' I read the words and reread them. I am no scholar, and don't pretend to be. However, I understand the importance of context when dealing with the ancient scriptures."

"And what was the context?"

"Daniel was describing one of his famous visions with descriptions of the four winds of heaven churning the sea, then this progression of fantastic beasts and lots of turmoil and tramping about. The beasts were destroyed and thrown into a river of fire. It was all very dramatic and I couldn't figure out where it was going until I came to the part about the *Ancient of Days* taking his seat on a throne, and the *son of man* approaching the Ancient of Days. I can tell you, Leah, that when I read those words the hair stood up on the back of my neck. I began to understand what the Galilean was saying and I was astonished and frightened all at the same time."

"You are saying – he was claiming to be a fulfillment of prophesy – maybe the Messiah!"

"That is what he seemed to be trying to tell me. He went on with another extraordinary statement. He said he had come into this world – those were his exact words – he had come into this world for judgment! Then he spoke one of his riddles: 'so the blind will see and those who see will become blind.'"

Leah was quiet for a few moments, then, "He was referring to you as the blind who will see, and to the rabbis and the Sanhedrin as those who will become blind."

"Yes and either he was a mad man or he was from G-d and came into the world, as he said, for the purpose of judgment which we assume is to be the role of the Messiah. But now he is dead! On the other hand I can't accept that he was a madman; he gave me my sight, after all. On the *other* hand the Messiah could not be subject to the whims and prejudices of mere men. His work, when he comes, will be unstoppable, his life eternal. So I am back to the beginning of my confusion."

Again, Leah was thoughtful, then, "Let's go back to Bartimaeus' words. He was told that his faith had healed him. Where is our faith? You and I of all people ought to have a measure of faith, considering where we are and where we came from. I'm no scholar, either; my father thought it a waste of time for me to learn to read. But I recall that when Abraham believed G-d it was credited to him as righteousness. That was all about faith, too, wasn't it? Maybe that's all that G-d expects of us now - that we believe. And why shouldn't we? We have proof!

Leah continued, "While I was still very young my mother told me stories from her childhood. She told me about a man called Job who was very rich, with many cattle and sheep. He owned large parcels of land for grazing and many barns for storing his grain.

He also had many children and grandchildren. He was known everywhere as a good man, sinless and obedient toward G-d in all his ways. According to this story there came a time when Satan approached G-d and challenged him to a duel: he would prove that Job's goodness and love for G-d were the result of G-d's having given Job so much prosperity. Take away the good things of his life and Job would turn his back on G-d. G-d accepted the challenge. In the weeks following, went my mother's story, Job's barns burned, his livestock were lost, the house collapsed on his children and grandchildren and they were killed, and finally Job himself was struck down with a terrible disease.

"In my mother's version of the story Job complained and cried bitterly to G-d, the way we all do sometimes: 'Why me?' In this account there followed many discussions about the power and purpose of G-d, unknowable to man. 'Where were you when I created the great monster of the deep,' G-d asked rhetorically, and so on. Of course Job had no comeback to G-d. The moral of this story, my mother told me, was simply that we are in no position to understand the ways and purposes of the Master of the Universe. How shall we substitute our wisdom for his? How shall we question the One who created us?

"Putting together my mother's lesson with the Galilean's words spoken to Bartimaeus, maybe all we can conclude is that G-d changed our lives for His own purposes, and His purposes are beyond our understanding."

Leah continued, "You said at the beginning of this discussion that the truth depends on what we believe it to be but if belief does not follow proof, where are we? It's interesting - all those people whose lives he seems to have touched and changed, and all the people who seem to have been witnesses to his work, yet we all seem to have trouble believing what was right in front of us. Yes, he is dead and maybe the lepers are clean and maybe not, and maybe Lazarus and his sisters are alive and well somewhere and maybe not. And maybe Bartimaeus of Jericho has forgotten his faith in his late years. But you can see and I have lived a life of joy. The innkeeper said he would believe in miracles when one happened to him. It may be hard to believe based on someone else's experience but we have our own experience. What more do we need?"

"Leah, my weaver-wife. You have become a philosopher. I got my sight but you are the one with vision. First the man from Galilee gave me my eyes, then he supplied me with a wife who sees truth."

❧

Chapter 20

THE PUPIL'S ACCOUNT

I was in one of Michael's first classes. There were twelve of us boys, all age six. We came into his classroom that first day expecting to be confronted with rules and warnings of severe punishment for inattention, tardiness, failure to learn and other such sins according to what we had been told by our older brothers. Instead Michael pulled up a chair, sat down with us and began talking to us as though we were intelligent human beings able to understand without threat. He went around the circle of students asking names, inquiring about families and interests while telling us a few things about himself.

Finally he said, "Boys, we are going to learn *together.*" It was only some years later that I understood that he meant those words literally. Because he had only recently gained his sight he was just learning to read and write and was only a little ahead of us. And that was how it was for the next several years. He taught himself vocabulary, the rules of sentence construction, syntax, punctuation, idiomatic forms and so forth always in time to pass it on to us.

Michael was never a pedantic schoolmaster. He could always find something of interest to share with us, probably because he was discovering so much of the world for himself. He would begin talking about the different trees and flowers growing in our area. Had we studied the colors, he would ask. Had we noticed how many shades of green there are in nature?

One day one of the boys asked if it was true that Michael used to be blind. While we all held our breath at this bold approach, Michael thought for a minute then sat down among us and began to talk about his years without sight. To demonstrate what it was like he instructed us to tie blindfolds around our eyes, then challenged us one by one to find our way across the schoolroom. It became a game; each of us would work our way through strategically located obstacles until we had learned the route and could walk from one side of the room to the other without stopping and without bumping in to anything. "That is how it is, boys. You learn to cope and you learn to use your minds in order to survive in the world. It is no different for you now: you can see but you must still learn to go through life without crashing into things and upsetting people."

When we laughed at his expressive way of speaking, his eyebrows bouncing up and down in time with his words, he would laugh along with us. Master Michael's schoolroom was always full either of the sound of boys reading, or of Michael speaking with his own brand of enthusiasm that caught us all up in its excitement, or with laughter - as much Michael's as ours.

In a lifetime of learning I have never had another teacher like him. In short he taught me to love study and learning and one more thing: I learned from that man the joy and excitement of discovery and have been seeking new things to discover and study ever since. It is clear to me now that his first 25 years of blindness forged in him the gift of wonder at everything he encountered later in life – so that he could pass it on to me!

By the time we had studied with Michael for a few years he had broadened our education beyond mere grammar. He said we should learn to appreciate the world around us and to understand people. He took us on what he called field trips. We would go out into the countryside where he would point out the "wonders of nature" then give us a little lecture about the history of our people and our connection to the land and how we had always had to fight for our place in it. We should understand that it was not always so peaceful for the Hebrews; yes, we were under the yoke of the Romans now but there was no fighting and no reason we should ever have war again. It was a matter of mutual respect, he told us. The Romans don't care who we worship; their only concern is their control of this part of the world. As long as we pay taxes and mind our business they will let us live our own lives and keep peace in the neighborhood. This simple view prevailed throughout Michael's lifetime, I am happy to say.

As we approached our *bar mitsvah* Michael tried to prepare us for the time we would be adults. We must understand people he said. What people say and what they mean may be two different things. We must watch their faces and their bodies for clues to their thinking. He would take a pose with his arms folded tightly to his body, lean back a little and look with a scowl past us, over our shoulders and ask us to guess what he was thinking. Then, holding that pose he would say something pleasant and ask if his expression matched his words. This, to us ten-year old boys, was craziness but we loved the game and we played along with him. I remember that lesson now 30 years later, as I carry on with my business in the marketplace.

At the end of a field trip, late in the afternoon, Michael would take us to his home where his wife would have prepared a treat for us. His wife's name was Leah and we loved her. She had the most beautiful eyes I have ever seen, before or since, and she spoke to us the way Michael did, as though we were adults. They never spoke down to us, but assumed we would understand them and could carry on an intelligent conversation.

We would be eating cookies and she would suddenly turn to me and say, "Now. Malachi. What have you learned since the last time we spoke?" I would tell her about something Michael had told us and she would purse her lips, think about it and allow that yes, that was one of Michael's theories. Then she would ask me my opinion; did I agree with Michael? If I said yes she would challenge me; had I really thought about it? If I said no, she would smile and ask for my reasoning, which she would listen to carefully; then, if she had a different view she would say so. She never patted us on the head. We always ended up in a lively conversation that was sometimes a debate and sometimes a rambling commentary on current events or history or the culture of our people. Those were the best times of my life up until then and very little that has happened to me since can match the hours I spent as a ten-year old with Michael and his bright, gentle wife. At about that time we began our study at the next level, the *beth midrash*, the so-called house of learning where we were introduced to an understanding and development of *halakhah*, Jewish law. According to Moses it was G-d's will that His commandments "…are to be upon your hearts. Impress them on your children. Talk about them when you sit at home and when you walk along the road, when you lie down and when you get up." So we began to spend our hours in the "house of learning" that was a dark room with little more than tables and benches and lecterns and several copies of *Sefer Torah*, the precious words of Moses scribed on a scroll of parchment.

Not only did we memorize long passages of the sacred writings; we studied the rabbinical tradition called *mitzvoth*, over 600 commandments of restrictions and positive instruction. We were barely more than children by then and only a few of us developed the habit of talking about what we had learned as we walked along the road, when we lay down and when we got up. As for me I learned as much as was required but I was more interested in worldly matters than in lengthy debate over the difference between the written law and the oral law tradition in which were to be found many levels of interpretation not revealed by Moses at Mount Sinai over 1300 years before.

When we were no longer Michael's pupils some of us (I especially since I was Michael's best and favorite pupil) would still go to his house for cookies and tea and long conversations with him and Leah. As far as Michael was concerned we were still learning together. Now we could ask him what he thought about Moses' strange tales of the creation and the Garden and Adam and Eve and their children, and how G-d brought Eve out of Adams rib cage. For some of us these accounts were factual and literally true. Others of us, including me, doubted that such unnatural things could have happened. How much then, of Moses writings, could we trust, we asked? Michael listened to the skepticism of a few countered loudly by the determination of others who had learned from the cradle the factual accuracy of Moses' account of the creation of our world.

Although Michael had described his years of blindness to us he had never made an explanation of how he had gained his sight. We knew that something apparently miraculous had happened; it was whispered about among our parents that some unknown rabbi had done something to make it possible for Michael to see. But Michael had never ventured an explanation to us. Now we waited to see how he would respond to a contradiction of a natural order of things against what an all-powerful G-d might choose to do in His Eternal Plan. While Leah sat back with a little smile, Michael began to speak carefully.

"In the first place," he explained, "the creation that surrounds us is proof not only of the very existence of the Master of the Universe, but that He is capable of doing in the natural world whatever He wills and *however* He decides to do it. On the other hand we must remember that Moses was relaying an explanation of G-d's purposes to a people considerably less learned and sophisticated than we are today. It is understandable that the explanation might be presented in allegorical terms. Surely, in your studies you have learned that Moses dealt not only in history, genealogy, and the exposition of various types of law but in poetry, metaphor and allegory as well. It seems to me that you can read Moses explanation as allegorical or literal; either way it is Truth. The important thing to learn is that G-d had His own purposes and that He has communicated to us through Moses in language that could be understood by either the most primitive or the most modern of His people.

"One thing to remember, however: Never try to argue your understanding of the scriptures with someone holding a different view. It is an exercise in futility."

It occurs to me now looking back on that exchange, that Michael's explanation was acceptable if politically prudent. It was clear that he wanted to make no contradiction of the truths we had learned but that his own view was more pragmatic. I have often wondered how he reconciled his own experience of an apparent miracle with his more utilitarian view of scripture. I remember looking toward Leah at the end of Michael's dissertation. She still had that little smile as she offered me another cup of tea.

The more time I spent with Michael and Leah the more I realized how strong was their union. As Moses tells us "… a man will leave his father and mother and be united to his wife, and they will become one flesh." The principle was perfectly reflected in the relationship of those two people. Not only did they have an intellectual and spiritual bond that made it seem they were always in harmony; and not only did they each seem always to know what the other was thinking. They even seemed to have a kind of material union in which Leah's disability was complemented by Michael's physical strength while Leah provided clarity of vision of the real world that was sometimes lacking in Michael. At least that was Michael's explanation - that Leah had taught him to see more clearly but also not to rely solely on his new-found vision for an understanding of what was going on around him, but to use all his senses as well as his *common* sense. "Remember the words of Isaiah," Michael said. "'The Lord shall not judge by what His eyes see, or decide by what His ears hear; but with righteousness he shall judge…'"

I must admit to my impatience with Michael's habit of reinforcing his views with quotations from the scriptures. He had a formidable memory and he used it frequently but I was never sure that he wasn't showing off a little. Or perhaps he was trying to provoke me to a more careful consideration of views I was apt to accept too readily. This was a tactic I believe he learned from Leah as it was one of her favorite ways to get me into our freewheeling discussions on just about any subject.

Leah had a friend whom I never met but who Leah often referred to as a woman with a "unique view of our paternalistic society", as she said. The subject came up while I was discussing my intention to find a wife and the characteristics I should look for, and should I rely on my parents to find an acceptable mate for me? I should be careful, Leah told me. She had learned from her friend something about the attitudes of men in our culture toward women. The most important characteristics I should be alert to were not a woman's physical features but the values and strengths less apparent on examination. I could have pointed out to Leah and Michael that this was a principle best demonstrated by their own marriage – but I did not.

I was interested to know more about Leah's friend: What was her background and experience that gave her such wisdom? Now it was Michael's turn to sit quietly by with a little smile on his face as Leah lectured me about the courting process while refusing to go into details about her friend. It is true, however, that what Leah told me then changed my approach to the matchmaking process and I found myself being more particular in my acceptance of a potential wife. This caused some impatience in my parents who were anxious for me to find a mate and get on with my life. In any case, a few weeks after this conversation I learned from Michael that Leah's friend had left the area long ago and had moved to Caesarea, that great city on the sea coast. According to Michael the woman owned property there; it was her intention to relocate – something about a problem she had had here in Jerusalem. Of course, Caesarea is a major commercial center on the trading route between Tyre and Egypt and I suppose that the woman's property would provide her with a comfortable existence. (Who knows how she came to own such a valuable asset.)

What is most interesting to me is the coincidence: Here is a woman, a friend of the wife of a man who was the benefactor of the miraculous work of a Galilean rabbi, emigrating to a city where there has been such uproar over the public pronouncements of one of the followers of that same rabbi. A certain Saul of Tarsus has been traveling about the Judean and Mediterranean area proselytizing about the rabbi and actually declaring him to have been unjustly executed by the Romans at the insistence of the Sanhedrin. Now, according to what I have been hearing through my own business contacts, the Sanhedrin decided they have to kill this Saul character for his seditious conduct before he could return to Jerusalem and stir up even more trouble. It is all very complicated; Saul was, according to the report, also a Pharisee but had somehow fallen in with the sect claiming loyalty to the rabbi. Even worse, he had brought gentiles into the group!

The local Roman commander, who had Saul under a sort of protective custody, brought him to Felix the Roman governor in Caesarea. There was a trial there with a whole contingent of elders and lawyers and even the high priest testifying against Saul. Naturally, his accusers wanted Felix to transfer Saul into their control in Jerusalem but Saul, who I am told is also a wily lawyer, can also claim Roman citizenship for himself and made an appeal to Caesar! Felix took the easy way out and decided to send Saul to Rome. There were more hearings and appeals even involving Herod Agrippa II, so-called king and the Roman overseer of the Temple and the high priest. (Small world!) How Saul was able finally to slip out of the reach of the Sanhedrin there is no way of knowing, but as I understand it he was sent to Rome where he will probably lie around for months or years before he faces another trial. I suspect that the majestic Roman courts will not have much interest in a trumped up case of religious insurrection fifteen hundred miles away in a scruffy colony like Jerusalem. And that will be the last we hear of Saul.

As you can see my friendship with Michael and Leah, starting when I was only six years old and continuing into my adult years, had a profound effect on my own views and choices about life and how I should live it. Not only did they provide a model for me as I sought to build my own family, but my career in business began with my acquaintance with Leah's father. I went to work for him when I was eighteen. I was privileged to learn business practices from one of the most successful merchants in Jerusalem, and have followed that career quite successfully myself. By the time I was 30 I was in a partnership with Leah's father and took over the business two years later when the old man died. His estate, of course, went to Leah and Michael. By then I was intimately involved not only with Leah's father's business, but also with everything about the family's affairs.

Michael had little patience with or knowledge of financial matters and was only too glad to let me make necessary decisions regarding the transfer of assets and responsibilities. "Just straighten everything out and let me get on with my teaching," Michael told me, something I was pleased to do for the two people I loved above all else.

In those later years when I was no longer Michael's pupil, but had become a kind of counselor and friend I tried to understand how he had gained his sight. Michael would say little about it and when I asked Leah she said that if I were to learn anything about the incident I would have to learn it from Michael. But it was as though Michael had achieved an understanding that he could not communicate. He had long since given up any attempt to find an explanation in the experiences of others, nor could his study of the writings of Moses and the prophets give him understanding. He only said that what had happened, happened. It was apparently in G-d's purpose that he be born blind, then gain his sight at the hands of a man whose name he never knew. He no longer searched for a reason the rabbi was executed; it didn't matter. All that mattered was his understanding that G-d had a purpose, not only for him but for Leah as well. What more could any reasonable man ask?

During the months that Leah's fragile body finally began to fail Michael discovered a new dimension to his love for the crippled woman who had become the strength and support of his life. He retired from his teaching during those months as she lingered, bedridden and nearly helpless. They would talk for hours about their life and how G-d had blessed them; there was still laughter and joy in that house. Their many friends stood ready to help, sitting with Leah during those few hours Michael had to be away.

When Leah died it was as though Michael began to die, too. He became quiet and contemplative, preferring to be by himself, I think. I would visit him several times every week and he was always glad for my company but was just as satisfied to be alone with his thoughts and memories. Michael lived until, as he said, he was "full of years and ready to go." In one of our last conversations he assured me of a peaceful heart. He hoped his life had justified the miracle of his sight. He had always wanted to share the wonders of all he could see around him and felt specially blessed to have been given the opportunity to teach. I assured him that his life had been a blessing for me and for many men like me. But it was special for me, I told him, since I was always aware that I was the best of all Michael's pupils! Michael chuckled at that and allowed that, yes that was probably true and that thanks to him I had turned out pretty well in spite of my inflated ego.

Michael and Leah had been together for nearly fifty years. Michael had become a well-respected teacher of boys and young men who knew only a little about the miracle of his life; but he was a legend for a younger generation free of the doubts and envy of our elders. I always wanted to know more about the "legend." The more I thought about it as Michael approached the end of his own life, the more I felt the urgency of learning the details while Michael was still alive. I especially wanted to know how Michael reconciled the miracle performed for him by the Galilean rabbi, with the fact of the rabbi's execution.

"I cannot reconcile the irreconcilable," Michael told me. "All I know is that he changed life for Leah and me. For that we both loved the memory of the man."

What about this movement we hear about now, I wanted to know. There were people who actually believed the man was alive and had appeared to several of his closest friends only days *after* he had been put to death. Michael had no opinion on the truth of these reports. He told me of his research into the reports of other miracles besides his own, and the ambiguity of his findings. Michael and Leah had heard these new reports but had made no attempt to contact the Galilean's followers. "Those of us who were touched by the man will remember him for as long as we live," he said. "But in time, when we are gone, the memory will pass away also along with the living proof of his work. These enthusiasts will pass away as well and the whole episode will lose credibility and will be forgotten forever."

In the years since Michael's death I have occasionally come across people who knew people who were familiar with the sect of followers of the rabbi from Galilee. There has been some confusion about the man's name. I have heard Jeshua and Jesiah but Jesus-ben-Joseph is the name most people use in reference to him. He grew up in Nazareth they say, a small out-of-the-way town in the Galilee area. His vocational training was as a common laborer; it is unknown where he acquired the knowledge of a rabbi. And it's interesting that this mysterious miracle man, coming from such modest beginnings, should have been one to cause so great a commotion in a major city like Jerusalem. In any case all that happened many years ago and I agree with Michael's prediction that the rabbi and his followers will soon be forgotten as the world continues on at its own pace.

There you have it: That is what I know about Michael and his remarkable life. I myself am in confusion as to what it all means. Although I believe every word of Michael's tale, including his interviews with others who were touched by the mysterious rabbi, I am left to wonder as to the meaning. There must be a moral to the story. Michael often spoke of the difficulty people seem to have arriving at a place of belief in spite of the evidence of their own lives. Perhaps I am like the innkeeper who could only believe if it happened to him. On the other hand, knowing Michael and Leah so well for so long was like observing a miracle in itself. I will have to think about these things. I have plenty of time to sort it all out and arrive at my own conclusions.

Epilogue

In a construction of "Michael" I have named the unnamed beggar and have imagined his life along with a few others who appear in the Gospel accounts. I have taken some liberties in doing so but have been careful not to reinterpret or do injury to the message of the Gospels. I have presented the narrative as in contemporary, 21st century idiom since it is impossible to duplicate the speech of a first century Jewish culture.

I have assumed that due to the lack of reliable news sources in that day, much of what was happening was poorly understood by most people; it was even possible for a man like Michael to be touched by the hand of God, as it were, and not even know His name.

I have respected the Jewish preference, in their respectful awe of the Creator, not to spell out His name but to use the term G-d in reference to Him. For Hebrew terminology I have found a wealth of information through Google and Wikipedia; I do not claim some special knowledge of rabbinic tradition and hope that no Jewish reader will take offense at my presumption.

The question of belief, and who has it and who does not, is a thread that runs through the tapestry of this story as surely as though woven by Leah herself. It is a question addressed by writers and philosophers in the past and continues to be an issue for each new generation, both within the Church and without. If we doubt that people could be in the presence of Jesus, yet deny Him; if it seems unlikely that Bartimaeus could lose the wonder of his own restored sight; and if we would rather not believe that a couple could live their whole adult lifetime satisfied with a partial understanding of the miracle of his sight and their marriage, then we have forgotten the lessons of our own lives and the countless examples of the discouraged redeemed and those who have lost or abandoned their faith.

We ought also to allow for the fact that Michael and his contemporaries did not have Paul's letters for an explanation of Jesus' life and purpose, nor did they have the advantages we enjoy of two thousand years of theological review, debate and testing of the New Testament. Yet for all of that, there persists in twenty-first century Christendom a wide variety of interpretations and beliefs.

The Way has endured. People have come to faith without miracles like Michael's. The question why some believe and others do not will persist as long as we are allowed free will.

About the author

Robert W. Foster is a retired civil engineer. He graduated from the University of Vermont in 1955 and served in the United States Air Force where he completed pilot training in 1958. He practiced as a consulting engineer in the Framingham, Massachusetts area until his semi-retirement in 1992. In his retirement he continued to provide consulting services in construction review, while providing dispute resolution services, and writing frequently for technical publications. He served as president of the *Federation Internationale de Geometre* from 1999 to 2002. He has three sons and two grandsons. His wife of 47 years, Margot, died in 2001. He lives in Hopkinton, Massachusetts.